I Dreamed of the person inside
By
Charles M. Kemp

Chapter 1

Marie was born in a small town with five brothers, two younger than her and three older. They attended school together while growing up, but then the three oldest brothers moved to another state after graduation. Marie played all the games that her brothers played, including tree climbing and rock throwing on the railroad tracks, she wrestled with them from time to time and most of the time she even dressed like they did. Other students often provoked her, calling her a tomboy, and unable to resist being provoked, she got into a lot of fights. Marie wanted to have girlfriends but other girls her age would see her playing with her brothers and would consider her too rough to take on as a girlfriend. She was spoiled as the only girl in the family, and most of the time the family would let her have her way about things around the house. While watching television, she wanted to be the prettiest lady in the movies, but she knew that in order to be the woman she desired to be, she would have to change her lifestyle. Marie's parents had wealthy friends who would come to visit, not often, but when they came they dressed really well. Marie would admire the fine dresses and suits that her parents' friends wore and she wanted to be able to dress accordingly. In her quiet moments she lay in her room and imagined a life of physical beauty, spiritual greatness, pride, success, and wealth. When she was seventeen and in her last year of high school, Marie realized that it would soon be time for her to enter the world. Her parents were strict with her. They required that she attend church and church activities regularly and keep the house clean, but she wasn't allowed to date or have boyfriends at the house. She was permitted to visit and receive girlfriends, though, and she was bitter.

One evening when Marie came home from school, she put her books away and said to her mother, "I've decided to join the army after graduation."

"I don't think joining the army is a ladylike thing to do. Why don't you consider attending a college and becoming a nurse?" her mother asked.

Marie snapped back, "I know what I want to do," and hurriedly left the room. That evening, when her father and mother were alone in the kitchen, her mother told her father about Marie wanting to join the army. "What?" he yelled. "I don't want to hear that mentioned in this house again. No daughter of mine is going to join the army, and that's that." Her father was hung up on the old-fashioned notion that a female's place was in the home, having and raising children. Marie overheard the conversation from her bedroom and decided that the time had come to rebel. A few evenings later, Marie was at church and overheard some friends talking about sneaking out to a friend's house for a party. *This is it*, she thought, and she went with them.

At the party, a young man by the name of John Baker approached her and introduced himself.

"May I get you something to drink?" John asked, glancing shyly into her eyes. "Sure," said Marie. "I'll have a glass of punch."

In a moment he was back with the punch. John stared at her while she drank. He finally

asked her if she would like to dance. Marie said yes, and he took her hand and led her politely to the dance floor. He held her in his arms, and they strolled across the floor in slow motion. Marie felt the heat from their bodies. She laid her head on his chest and could hear his heart beating. They held each other gently as John softly whispered adorations in her ear. When the music stopped, John said, "Can we talk on the patio? I'd like to show you something."

They made their way through the crowd to the patio. As they walked outside, John looked into Marie's eyes and then slowly kissed her. She enjoyed the taste of his mouth. Marie found herself wanting to feel more of his tongue, to taste it and suck on it. Though she felt herself getting swept away by his passion, Marie gained control of herself and said softly, "It's getting late, and I should be getting home or my parents will be worried."

"May I give you a ride home?" John asked.

"No thank you. I came to the party with my girlfriend, and we're leaving together."

"Then may I have your phone number?" John asked. "Okay, but don't call too late at night."

Marie arrived back home on time and snuck into the house quietly so her parents wouldn't see the look of satisfaction on her face and know that she hadn't been to church. For four nights John phoned Marie. He told her about his feelings and how much he wanted to be with her again, to look into her eyes and kiss her lips. Marie listened and imagined how delightful it would be if she was there with him while he said those things to her. She dreamed how life would be if she and John could be together forever.

One night John called and said that his need to see her had become unbearable. Filled with passion and more than a little rebelliousness, Marie said, "I'll see you tomorrow night at seven." John's parents were out of town for the weekend, so they arranged to meet at his house.

The next evening Marie told her parents that she was going to church. She walked hurriedly to John's house and knocked softly on his door. John answered, and Marie entered the house. The door closed, and the moment they were behind it, John put his arms around her and started kissing her and stroking her back. The only thing Marie thought of was how good his body felt against hers. They stood kissing, pressing against each other's bodies. John placed his hands on her buttocks, pulling her closer to him. He began to nibble on her ear and placed his hand on her breasts, squeezing gently. He moved to kiss her neck and slowly pulled up one side of her halter-top and bra, exposing her breast. He lowered his mouth further and began to suck on her nipple. Marie was nervous, but she moaned with pleasure. John moved his hand up her leg and under her skirt, rubbing between her thighs until he reached her vagina. Then he pulled her panties aside and touched her with his fingers. He slipped a finger inside her, and she began to thrust forward, moving in a circular motion as if she wanted his finger to go deeper. Marie had never been with a boy in this way before, but she knew what he wanted. Even though she felt pleasure, she forced his finger away from her, saying, "No, John. I'm afraid. I'm just not ready yet."

John took a deep breath and said, "It's okay. I can wait." Then he kissed her again more aggressively.

Marie slowly pushed away and said, "I have to go now. It's getting late." "I'll call you tomorrow." He kissed her and said goodnight. That night, she laid quietly in her bed, thinking of

being with John, only John,
Forever. As the weeks went by, John called less and less often. He would call her one night, and then it would be two or three nights before he would call again. Marie became

Worried, so one night when he phoned she asked, "What's wrong? Why don't you call me the way you used to?"

"Nothing's wrong," he replied. "I've just been busy with my studies. I'll try to call you more."

"I didn't mean to pry," said Marie, "but I was beginning to think you were losing interest in me."

"Oh, no," John said. "Its just school."

They chatted for a little while longer, said goodnight, and hung up. The next day in school during a class break, Marie noticed that John was standing in the hallway talking with another girl. It was her friend, Patty, so she thought nothing of it. Every day after that, Marie would find them standing in the hallway talking during a class breaks. Marie finally approached them.

"Hi, Patty, John," she said. But before she could utter another word, the bell rang. "Well, I guess I'll see you guys later," Patty said, and they went off in different
Directions. After the school day ended, Marie waited for John at the exit. She waited until the last student left the building, but John never came. Later she found out that he and Patty had both made excuses and left early. After that day John avoided Marie during class breaks, and she didn't get to see him after school.

Marie was confused and upset. She didn't want to deal with the thought of John being with someone else. One day after school, she decided she would walk along the street where John lived and possibly stop to see him. Just as she turned the corner onto John's street, she saw him and Patty standing on the porch, hugging, kissing, and caressing each other as if they didn't care if the whole world saw them. Marie cared. She stopped in her tracks when she saw them. Tears fell from her eyes as she turned and walked away.

For days she remained miserable, snapping at her parents and yelling at her brothers. She felt cheated when she thought of all the times that she and John had said that they loved each other over the phone, the times when they went to the park and chased after her brothers when they teased them about being in love. She thought of how eager she had become to give up her virginity to him.

At school one day, Marie heard about a house party that the whole class was invited to. She went out that night under the pretext of going to church, but before she got there, she went to the party. When she walked in the door, she felt lonely, thinking of what it was like when she met John at the first party she went to. Fighting the feeling, she began to mingle until she came upon a door, which she thought was the bathroom. As she opened the door, her eyes began to burn from all the smoke, and she couldn't see who was inside. There was a scent that she had never smelled before. She stood there in a daze, but being blinded by the smoke and the tears in her eyes, she couldn't find the knob to let herself out. After feeling around with her hands, she reached the knob and let herself out, coughing. She rushed to the refreshment table for water. After drinking for a moment,

the coughing cleared up, and she began to feel as if she didn't have a worry in the world. She felt that the sky was beneath her feet.

She wanted to dance, so she approached an attractive guy who seemed to have some of John's features and asked him for a dance. He, of course, accepted. She took his hand and led him to the dance floor. The music played softly, and he held her in his arms as they moved in motion with the music.

In her mind, Marie was in John's arms. She pressed her body against the boy, moving her hips in a circular motion. Her partner pressed forward also. Marie could feel his erection; it was as if it penetrated her clothing. The dance floor was crowded, and they stood still, pressing their bodies against each other, as the music played slowly. Marie opened her legs as if to invite the erection in. They looked into each other's eyes, and their lips met.

Thinking of John, Marie kissed him and tasted his tongue. When she sucked on it, she could feel his erection get harder. The music finally stopped. Marie seem dizzy, and the boy asked if he could take her home.

"Yes," she replied.

They left the party, got into his car, and drove away. He wanted to go for a drive, but Marie told him to take her home. She arrived home safely, thanked the boy, and went inside her house. Marie still didn't want to confront John about being with Patty; she felt shy and inexperienced. She didn't know what to do, only that her soul yearned for love and happiness.

One evening, sitting home alone, Marie thought of the way she had felt at the last party, how happy and worry-free she felt. She traced her actions at the party and came to the conclusion that the smoke she inhaled in the room was what made her feel that way. She wanted that feeling again. She went to her friend who gave the party and asked her about it. "Oh, some guys were just smoking pot and doing coke. You must have smelled that." She also told Marie how to get in touch with the guys. After school, Marie found one of those guys and asked where she could get some pot.

"Come with me to my apartment," he said. "I have some there." He assured Marie that his only interest was in smoking with her, so she trusted him and went to his apartment. Once they were inside, he locked the doors and windows and pulled down the shades.

"Don't worry. I'm doing this so no one will know that we're smoking," he said. "Oh, by the way, my name is Sam." Sam was a tall, skinny guy, who was neatly dressed. He had a long, brown ponytail and wore dark glasses. He turned on a red strobe light and pulled what looked like a cigarette from his pocket. He lit it with his lighter and puffed on it before passing it to Marie. "Puff on it," he said. "Inhale it like I did."

Marie tried to inhale. She started coughing at first, but within moments she was smiling and laughing.

"Can I have a drink of water?" she asked.

"Sure," Sam said, "but vodka's better when you smoke." He poured her a shot of vodka, and she swallowed it in one gulp. Even though it burned going down, she wanted more. It seemed to her that the more she drank, the better she felt. From that afternoon on, every day after school Marie

would go to Sam's apartment to smoke and drink.

Marie managed to graduate from high school and left home. She did not give up Sam's pot and booze. One day, after smoking and drinking at Sam's apartment, she was driving on the highway and came within inches of crashing head-on into an eighteen-wheeler. Screaming, she realized that her life was in danger and fought to gain control of the vehicle. She got back on her side of the road. For a moment only she swore that she would give up the pot and give up the booze, but like all promises made in despair, she couldn't keep it.

Having so few experiences against which to compare her current life, she was afraid to be around people when she wasn't drinking or drugging. Marie felt that there was no hope of handling her fears any other way. She didn't like it, but she excused it, saying she was the only girl in her family, and her parents wouldn't let her socialize enough with other girls her age. It was their fault she was afraid of being around certain people. Besides, she felt more comfortable with people whom she didn't care about, and it was a lot of fun, fun she deserved, getting into sordid affairs.

Through college, Marie more or less kept her life in order, and after getting her degree; she worked for a marketing firm. She enjoyed her job and was a very dedicated worker. She usually brought lunch and ate alone at her desk, but one day she decided to have lunch at the cafeteria in the building where she worked. As she sat at the table eating, a man walked over with his tray and said, "My name's Frank. May I join you?"

"My name's Marie. Be my guest," she said smiling.

He sat at the table across from Marie and began to eat. Frank was tall and muscular; he had blue eyes and a nice smile. There they sat, glancing at each other every now and then. Frank finally broke the silence saying, "Do you eat here every day?"

"No, today's my first time," Marie said.

Frank replied, "Normally I don't have lunch here either, but today I was really busy, and I got too hungry to go elsewhere." They talked for the remainder of the lunch hour. Before they went their separate ways, Frank said, "It's been nice dining with you. Maybe we can do this again when you have more time."

"Yes, maybe," Marie answered.

The next day before lunch, Frank phoned Marie at her office. "I called to ask if you'd like to have lunch with me today," he said.

"Sounds good. What time and where?" "How about the steak house downtown?"

"Okay," Marie replied, "but remember, I only have an hour." "Don't worry. I'll get you back to work on time. See you at eleven," he said. At
Exactly eleven o'clock, Frank picked up Marie. They got into his convertible and drove to the restaurant. When they arrived, Frank gave his name to the waitress, and they were escorted to a table. Marie excused herself and went to the ladies' room. In her purse she carried a contact lens case that contained cocaine. She used a long fingernail to scoop the powdery stuff from the lens case, and she snorted it up her nose. When she returned she was feeling good.

"Frank," she said. "What's the occasion? Did you get a promotion or something?" "Oh, no, I

just felt like treating you to a nice meal at my favorite restaurant." They had lunch together every day for a month before Frank finally asked,
"Would you like to have dinner with me sometime? Go out on an official date?"

"Of course," said Marie. "Anytime."

They started seeing each other regularly. Frank called Marie at her office one Friday and asked, "How would you like to go away this weekend?"

"Really? Sounds good to me. I'd love to" she said.

"Just pack an overnight bag and leave the rest to me."

After work, they drove for about an hour and pulled into a luxurious resort in the New Orleans area. Frank asked her to wait in the car while he went in the office to get the Keys to their private cottage. They took their bags inside, freshened up, and got ready for dinner. Frank took Marie to a beautiful French restaurant with a courtyard in the French Quarter. They sat and smiled at each other while the live band played.

The waiter brought an expensive bottle of champagne to their table and poured it into their glasses. They toasted each other to celebrate a wonderful night together. They ate slowly, talked some, and stole glances at each other. Under the table, Marie pulled off her shoes and stroked every part of Frank's body that she could reach with her bare feet. She moved her seat next to his, and Frank rubbed her thighs with one hand. By the time they left, they could hardly keep their hands off each other. Back at the cottage, Frank went to the refrigerator and took out a bottle of champagne. He got two glasses and asked Marie to join him.

"Just a minute," said Marie. "I have to use the ladies' room." Marie grabbed her purse and went into the bathroom. She sat on the stool and
Pulled out the contact lens case. With her fingernail, she held a bit of cocaine to her nose and sniffed. Her eyes opened wide, and her toes curled and twitched. With a smile on her face, she returned to the bedroom where Frank sat waiting patiently. He handed her a glass. After a few sips he kissed her and, with his arms around her, he began to remove her clothes. Marie said with a soft voice, "Wait, I'll do it myself." She seem shy and inexperienced, but she had done this many times before. This secret, like so many other secrets of her life, she felt no desire to share with Frank. This was the way the game was played.

She removed everything except her bra and panties. She placed her hand in Frank's, and they toasted each other. They placed the glasses on the table and pushed and pulled each other to the bed, kissing and hugging. Marie reached back and removed her bra and then her panties. She pressed her body against him. Neither could wait any longer. Frank began to shower her with kisses. He tasted every inch of her body. Marie couldn't take anymore and reached an orgasm. Marie whispered to Frank, "Now it's my turn to pleasure you." She turned him over and returned the kisses he had given her before getting on top of him. She placed him inside her, holding him tightly with her hidden muscles, and moving up and down until they climaxed together.

At breakfast the next morning Frank said, "Did you enjoy yourself last night, sweetheart?"

Marie replied, "It was okay but no big deal."

A tense moment passed, and then Frank asked, "Is there anything I can do to show you how much I love you?"

"Well, you can start by telling me if I am the only woman you brought to this cottage and screwed?" Marie said. She needed a fix, and her attitude was changing. She excused herself from

the table and ran to the bathroom where she had another snort of cocaine. It was the last of the cocaine. Marie knew she had to get back home to restock.

When she returned, she said only, "I need a drink."

She grabbed the champagne from the refrigerator and began to drink greedily. Quickly, Frank left the table saying, "I'll start packing so we can get back home."

Frank and Marie remained silent as they drove on the interstate heading for home. When they reached Marie's house, she grabbed her bags and got out of the car without saying anything to Frank. She angrily slammed the door and walked into her house.

A few days went by before Frank called Marie at work. Marie told him that she was too busy to talk and hung up on him. One evening Frank drove to her house and knocked on the door. Opening the door and seeing that it was Frank, Marie said, "What do you want?"

"I love you," Frank said.

"Ha! Everybody loves somebody," she replied airily.

"Why are you saying all these crazy things to me?" Frank asked. "Does my love for you mean anything?"

When she didn't answer, Frank walked away saying, "Good-bye, Marie. I won't be back." Marie loved Frank, but she was having mood swings because she couldn't make contact with her supplier to get a fix of cocaine. She was almost out of control. Tears fell from Marie's eyes as she realized what she had done to Frank. She reached into the bar, pulled out a bottle of vodka, and drank.

"He loved me, and I drove him away," she murmured "Oh, God. Please help me change my life." She threw the bottle against the door and broke it. Then she cried until she fell asleep.

Chapter 2

One evening after work, Marie decided to stop at the local bar for a drink, as was her habit. The owner was cleaning off tables. Marie asked, "Where is the waitress?" The owner told her that the waitress wouldn't be in until later. Seeing that the owner needed help, Marie said, "Well, I'll help you with the tables before the place gets crowded. And she proceeded to clean the tables until they were all done. In return, her drinks were free for the rest of that night. Afterwards, she would occasionally clean off tables when the bar got busy and was short of help. She became good friends with the employees and the owner. She also became friends with customers who, from time to time, would borrow money from her. She was known at that bar as a person who would do whatever she could to help people. Customers and friends who frequently visited the local bar were happy to see Marie there because they knew they could talk to her about their problems and that she would listen, or pretend to listen, as they shared the cost of drinks. Sitting at the bar one night, Marie noticed a young man entering through the doors. He was tall, muscular, and good-looking.

"Good evening ladies and gentlemen," he said. He sat at the bar and ordered a beer. As he drank, Marie caught his eye. He turned to a customer sitting next to him and said, "My name's Robert Maxwell." He offered his hand.

The customer shook hands with Robert and replied, "Phillip. But everyone calls me Phil."

"I'm pleased to meet you," Robert said. Looking at Marie, Robert asked, "Do you know that lady sitting across the bar from us?"

"That's Marie. Would you like to meet her?"

"Yes I would," Robert replied, grinning. Robert asked the bartender to give Marie whatever she wanted to drink.

When the drink was delivered to her, Marie asked, "Who ordered this?" "The gentlemen sitting across from you," the bartender said.

Robert raised his glass as if to toast her, and Marie nodded as if to say thanks for the drink. Phil got up and walked over to where Marie was sitting and whispered in her ear, "Let me introduce you to him." Marie got up and followed Phil to the other side of the bar.

"Robert, this is Marie. Marie, this is Robert," Phil said. He took his seat again. Robert offered Marie his hand. She shook it, and he held hers as she stood next to him.

"Won't you sit at a table with me and have a drink?" Robert asked. "I'd like to get to know you better now that I'll be visiting here more often."

"Okay," Marie said, "but first, let me use the ladies' room." Robert got a table while Marie walked to the bathroom. When she returned, Robert ordered drinks for the both of them.

"I'll buy the next round," Marie offered. They sat sipping their drinks and glancing into each other's eyes as they talked.

"What do you do for a living?" Marie asked.

"Well," Robert started, "I retired from the military recently, and now I'm thinking about what I want to do next."

Like Marie, Robert had been a victim of a past relationship that had left him in despair. One night some years earlier, he walked out of a bar onto the sidewalk. He turned his head left and right to decide which direction to go. When he turned to the left, he noticed a woman walking toward him. As she came closer, he gazed at her from her long legs to her beautiful face. She wore a white mini-skirt that fit her fine, shapely body, and she had long black hair that flew with the breeze as she walked. As she came even closer, Robert looked into her eyes. From a distance he saw a gleam and then a sparkle. Still staring into her eyes as she walked by him, he said, "Lady, I don't know where you're going, but I sure would like to come along."

Robert was surprised when she turned around, walked up to him, and asked, "What did you say?"

Robert nervously explained, "As I looked into your eyes, I knew I wanted to spend some time with you, and I couldn't stand here and let you pass me by without saying something."

"My name's Susana. I'm going to the Shalimar Lounge to find my sisters. Then we're going

to get something to eat."

"Please excuse my bad manners. My name is Robert. May I join you?" "Sure, but if you have a girlfriend tailing you, then don't bother because I don't want to be accused of trying to take some other woman's man."

"Oh, no, I'm unattached."

They walked together toward the Shalimar, and on the way they met Susana's Sisters.

"We were just coming to look for you two," Susana said. "I'm starving. Let's go have breakfast. Oh, sorry," she said to Robert. She introduced him to her sisters.

"My car is across the street," Susana said.

"I don't think it would be too comfortable to take one car," Robert said. "Why don't I bring my car, and Susana can ride with me?"

"Fine with me. Let's go," Susana said.

They drove their cars to the coffee shop. When they arrived, Robert and Susana sat in a booth across from each other with one of Susana's sisters next to each of them.

Susana's sister noticed them staring at each other, as if neither could tear their eyes away. "Susana," one sister said, nudging her, "Why are you looking at him like that?"

"Robert is looking at me," Susana giggled.

Robert said to her sisters, "I've fallen in love with your sister, and I don't care if the whole world knows it." Susana blushed as the waiter brought their breakfast, and they all laughed.

For Robert it was love at first sight. He suddenly lost his appetite and couldn't eat another bite. Before they left the cafe, Robert asked Susana where she lived.

"In Georgia, but we're in Alabama visiting our aunt for a while." "How long will you be staying?" asked Robert.

"I don't know yet," she answered. "You see, my aunt's in the hospital recovering from an operation that she had two days ago, and we're going to stay here until she gets back on her feet. We're going to the hospital tomorrow afternoon to visit her. Would you like to come along?"

"Yes," Robert said. "What time do I pick you up?" "Oh, that won't be necessary," said Susana. "We'll pick you up." Robert gave Susana the phone number and address to his trailer. Not wanting to leave, he held her hand, and her eyes seem to glitter as he told her how happy he was that he had met her.

"I feel the same," Susana said, as she walked toward the car. Robert rushed over and opened the door for her. After she got inside, he closed it and leaned in the window. Susana kissed his cheek and said, "Thanks for breakfast. I'll call you tomorrow."

Susana drove away, and Robert stood there for a few minutes to regain his senses. After a moment he turned, got into his car, and drove home. He sat on the corner of his bed with visions of

Susana in his head. Then he shouted, "I'm in love!" and fell back on his bed. Smiling at the ceiling, he fell asleep.

The next day was Saturday, and Robert decided to get his car washed. He got up around noon and, with Susana on his mind, rushed off to wash his car. He listened to music as he cleaned the car and thought of Susana. He could hardly wait until she called. When he finished, he rushed home, straightened his house, turned the TV on, and sat patiently by the phone as he gazed at the screen. Still full of joy and love, he didn't eat. The only thing he wanted was to see Susana. Robert fell asleep while watching TV; the ringing of the telephone woke him. Robert quickly grabbed it and said, "Hello?"

"Hello," Susana replied cheerfully. "Is this Robert?"

Clearing his throat, Robert answered, "Hi, Susana, it's me. How's your day going?"

"Just fine. Are you still going to the hospital with us today?" "Oh, yes. What time?"

"I'll be over in about an hour to pick you up," Susana said. "Okay," said Robert, "I'll see you then."

Susana picked Robert up, and they went to the hospital. When visiting hours were over, they walked to Susana's car holding hands. Suddenly Robert jumped up clicking both of his heels together. "I feel great!" he shouted.

Susana looked at him in astonishment. "What brought all that on?" she asked. "Well," said Robert, smiling, "you know what they say. When people fall in love, they go crazy."

"In that case, leave room for me because I'm crazy about you, too," Susana laughed. They kissed as they held hands, and then got into the car and drove away.

"Let's go by my house. I have something important to tell you," Robert said. They drove to Robert's house and went inside. "Make yourself comfortable," Robert said. "Just help yourself to anything you see." He rushed into the bathroom. When he returned, he asked, "May I get you something to drink?"

"Sure," Susana replied. As he poured two glasses of wine, Susana walked over to the couch and sat down. Robert turned on some soft music and dimmed the lights. Then he walked across the room, reached out to Susana, and asked, "May I have this dance?"

Susana blushed and said, "Of course."

Robert assisted her in getting up from the couch. He held her in his arms as they stepped slowly to the music. The sound wrapped itself around them in harmony with the thrilling sensations and trembling emotions derived from caressing each other. They sighed as they touched. Susana began to moan as Robert's body pressed against hers. He looked into her eyes, and Susana couldn't resist as Robert kissed her lips. Button by button, Robert opened her silk blouse, finally letting it slide to the floor. He felt the smoothness of her skin as he stroked her neck and shoulders. Susana broke their kiss and looked into Robert's eyes as she unbuttoned his cotton shirt. Robert ran his fingers through her long black hair and held the back of her head as she kissed his chest. He stroked her back as he reached for her skirt. He unzipped it and pulled it below her hips. The skirt fell to the floor, and she pushed it aside with her foot.

Susana began to unbuckle Robert's belt. She unzipped his pants and let them fall to the floor. Robert stepped out of them. Susana sunk slowly to her knees and explored his genitals with her lips. Robert held her head up and looked at her face. Swelling with desire, he carried her in his arms and gently laid her on his bed. She opened her legs and invited him in. He began Finger massaging her as he gave her more kisses, listening to her for approval to explore more. He was doing what he thought she wanted him to do. She could feel Him. His fingers guided the way for his tongue and his kisses; her back was arched expecting him to love her with every part of his body. Kiss me right there she murmured. Oh baby, I am so glad that you do what you do to me. You make me feel sexier than I have ever felt before. He knew that her breast were sensitive so he nibbled on them like they were exotic candy, first the left, then the right. She massaged his shoulders and whispered into his ear lets go baby, let your hands lead the way through the slopes of our lovemaking and let your tongue be the navigational tool to find my needs, he held her close, for that climactic moment. He kissed her again and asked if she wanted it. She shed a single tear as she realized that the goodness was about to be hers. I know what you want, you have told me with your kisses and your tongue. Then he gently parted her legs, he kissed her thighs again and headed to the playground of her love, she began to whisper to him and tell him that she enjoyed watching him do what he was doing. Please, please baby, I am ready. I want you to have all of me she said. He parted her thighs again and began stroking her as she arched her back to receive him and they screamed with pleasure.

When it was over, she kissed Robert goodnight, and went home.

Chapter 3

The next day Robert sat quietly in his trailer thinking that soon it would be time for Susana to go back to Georgia. He wished there was something he could do to keep her from leaving, but to no avail. Before Susana left, she gave Robert her phone number in Georgia and told him to keep in touch. Robert called Susana every night for days, telling her how much he loved her and wanted to be near her. When his phone bill came and he saw the cost, Robert thought that something must be done. He called Susana and asked if she could come back to visit him. Susana explained that she had one-week vacation time from her job the following week and that she would come. They chatted for a while and as always, ended with the words "I love you."

A week later, just as Robert got home from work, the phone rang. "Hello," said a soft voice. "This is Susana. I'm at the airport. Can you come pick Me up?"

Robert answered, "Really? You're really here? I'm on my way right now." "Okay. I'll be waiting at exit eight." Robert hung up without saying good-bye, Hurried to his car, and drove to the airport. When he arrived, he saw Susana standing near the exit.

"What a beautiful sight," he thought. They hugged and kissed on the sidewalk as people stared and smiled.

"You just don't know how happy I am to see you," Robert said. "So am I," said Susana. "I missed you so much."

Two days passed and Robert said to Susana, "I don't think I could stand for you to leave

again. Why don't you move in here and get a job so we can be together?"

"Are you proposing to me?" Susana asked.

"Yes, I am. Will you marry me?" "I accept," Susana said, smiling.

They got their blood tests and were married by the justice of the peace within the week. At that time, Robert worked for the government as a maintenance man. When he went to work, he told everyone in his crew about Susana and how they had gotten married.

"How long have you known her?" asked one of the workers. "Three months," said Robert, "but it seems as if I've known her all of my life." After weeks of searching for work, Susana was unable to find suitable
Employment.

"Don't worry," Robert assured her, "I'll get a second job to help take care of the both of us." Robert got a second job as a security guard. He was required to wear a gun. He purchased a forty-four-magnum pistol and wore it to the security job each day.

Months went by, and Robert grew tired and frustrated from the two jobs and long hours at work. He would come home angry, aggravated, and grouchy. When Susana tried to cheer him up, he would yell at her. When he calmed down, he would apologize, saying, "I don't know what came over me."

"You're just tired," Susana said. "You've been working too many hours. You should quit one of your jobs. We can make it until I find work."

"No," Robert said. "I'll be all right."

One day after working long hours, Robert decided not to go directly home. He stopped at a bar for a drink. He sat at the bar drinking shot after shot, until the bartender refused to sell him any more alcohol. Robert staggered to his car and drove home. When he reached the door, he couldn't find his keys so he knocked. Susana was asleep in the back bedroom and couldn't hear him. He began to knock harder, but still she couldn't hear him.

"Open the damn door!" he yelled. "Who's in there with you? Open this damn door, or I'll break it down." Susana woke up and rushed to the living room, and when she opened the door, Robert slapped her in the face. He yelled, "What were you doing in here? Why didn't you open the door? Were you busy with someone else?" He went from room to room yelling uncontrollably.

Susana sat on the couch, holding her bruised face in her hands and murmured, "Why are you doing this?"

Finally Robert fell across the bed and went to sleep, and Susana slept on the couch. The next morning Robert got up and went to the living room to look for her.

Susana was still asleep on the couch. He saw the bruises on her face. Tears ran down his cheeks as he realized what he had done. Feeling unworthy of her, he slipped on his shoes quietly and left for work.

After work, unable to face his wife at home, Robert went to the bar again. He drank until the bartender cut him off, and then he staggered to his car and went home. When he arrived this time,

he used his key. When he opened the door, he saw Susana standing across the room, dressed in her robe as he had left her that morning. Her eyes were swollen and red from crying. She approached him, grabbed his arm with one hand and punched and scratched his face with the other. Robert, still staggering from his drinking, pushed her away.

"I'm sorry. I'm sorry. I didn't mean to hurt you last night," he said. Susana turned her back to him and began to weep. Robert took off his jacket and Gun belt. He intended to take the gun out of the holster and place it in the drawer. He reached down to his side and pulled the gun from his holster, not realizing that his finger was on the trigger. As he placed the gun on the table, it went off. Time stood still as he turned to Susana.

Susana hesitated for a moment before she cried, "Oh, my God!" Robert looked at her hip, the place where the bullet had gone in. He ran over to Her, picked her up, and placed her in his car to take her to the hospital. Robert was driving well over the speed limit when he passed a police car on the road to the hospital. The officer turned his lights on for Robert to stop, but Robert paid no attention. He kept driving as fast as he could. However, farther up the road another police car was blocking the way, so Robert had no choice but to stop. A policeman came swiftly to his window and yelled, "Get out of the car!"

Robert started to get out, explaining, "My wife has been shot." The policeman looked at Susana and, seeing that she was bleeding, called an Ambulance. The ambulance came and Robert rode to the hospital with his wife. The doctor treated the wound and said that Susana was lucky. It was a clean wound that penetrated the left side of her buttocks, and she would be all right in a few days.

A week went by, and Susana was discharged from the hospital. Robert stayed home from work to change her bandages and take care of her. He couldn't help but feel hurt, ashamed, and embarrassed about what he had done. Susana got well, and Robert returned to work.

One night, as Robert lay drunk and asleep, Susana gathered up some of her clothes and left. When Robert woke up the next day, he reached over to hug Susana, but she wasn't there. He called out her name because he thought she was somewhere in the house, but there was no answer. He got up and looked in every room. He looked in the closet and saw that some of her clothes were missing. It was then that he realized she had left him. With tears in his eyes, he sat on the bed wishing that there was something he could do to make her come back, but he had no idea where she had gone.

As the days passed, Robert had no interest in work. He felt as if his insides had been torn out. About a year later, he received a divorce decree from his wife who was living in Georgia. Robert granted her the divorce.

Still hurt and running from himself, trying to escape the reality of being divorced and unloved, he searched for ways to keep busy. He traveled for a while, using truck

Driving as an excuse. He began to feel the need for love. Soon he returned home, and that's when he met Marie.

"What do you do for a living?" Robert asked.

"I work in marketing for the Waco Company at Maxwell Field Air Force Base," said Marie.

"Do you like it, or did you just take the job for the money?"

"Both," Marie said. "When the work day's over, I come to the bar for a drink. At the present time I'm not seeing anyone, and I don't want to stay home and be bored."

Robert smiled and asked, "What happened in your last relationship?" Marie gave a few sad details. "I don't care to discuss this anymore. I still get upset When I talk about it."

"Well," Robert said, "I'm not seeing anyone at the present time either." "What happened during your breakup?" Marie asked.

"It's a long story. I'll tell you about it sometime," Robert said. Before Robert left the bar, he asked Marie if he could give her a ride home. "I'll be okay," said Marie. "I live just around the corner."

"Fine, I'll walk with you." Robert walked with Marie to her doorstep. "Could I call you sometime?"

"Yes, I'd like that." After she gave Robert her number, Robert said goodnight and went inside.

A day went by. As Robert lay in his bed, he had visions of Marie's sweet face. He called her and invited her out to the bar, and soon they were meeting there every weekend. One night, Robert said, "I need to tell you how I feel about you. I think you're a beautiful and charming person, and each time we're apart, I long to be with you. It's getting harder and harder during the week, waiting for the weekend to ask you out so I can be with you. You're in my dreams, and you're becoming the light of my life."

Marie blushed as she held Robert's hand. "My feelings are strong for you, but I'm just not ready to commit yet. There are some things that I need to get cleared up before I get involved in another relationship."

"Okay, I can wait," said Robert. "And who knows, maybe you'll commit to being with me for the rest of your life."

As the days went by, Marie and Robert saw more and more of each other. They fell deeply in love, to the point that neither could bear being apart from the other. During a discussion one day, Marie said, "Why don't we just move in together?"

"No," Robert said. "I don't believe in shacking up. If I'm going to live with a woman, we must be married." His words ended that discussion.

Whenever Marie wasn't with Robert, she would find herself slipping away to use cocaine because she didn't want to deal with the emptiness and loneliness that she felt without him. It was then that Marie decided that she needed help. Marie went to one of her old friends, Julia. During a conversation about other friends who had been on drugs, they talked about a women's drug rehabilitation center downtown. Marie hoped that someone could transform her personality and help her conquer the cocaine and alcohol temptation. She thought that this would be a battle that she could win only with professional help.

That night when Marie went home, she could hardly sleep thinking about the drug addicts that she saw in the alleyways, how awful they looked, and how they begged for nickels and dimes to support their habits. She pictured herself having to sell her body to support her drug addiction.

And when she could no longer sell her body then what? She also wondered what her family would think if they knew that she was on drugs. But most of all, she wondered what Robert would think, or if being on drugs would cause her to lose him. Before Marie went to sleep, she came to the decision that regardless of what others thought, she was going to attend the rehabilitation center.

The next morning, Marie went to the center. When she arrived, she told the counselor that she had a drug and alcohol problem and wanted to get help with it, but she didn't want anyone to know. The counselor replied, "One of the first steps in curing an addiction is to admit to yourself and your loved ones that you have a problem."

"I admit to you and myself that I have the problem, but I'm just not ready to admit to anyone else until I've tried to overcome it," Marie confessed.

"Well," the counselor said, "since you're an adult, I see no reason why we can't keep your problem under wraps, at least for a while. So let's get started. I want you to check into the center on Friday. At that time you'll be admitted as a patient and expected to stay until you feel that you can deal with life on the outside without having to use drugs or alcohol. You'll be observed to determine the seriousness of your addiction before the rehabilitation process begins." Marie agreed to these terms. She thanked the counselor for seeing her and returned home.

That night before she was able to sleep, she thought of different stories to tell her family and Robert. She dreamed up a story about going on a vacation for thirty days and told Robert and her family that they wouldn't be able to contact her because she wasn't sure where she would be staying. She told them that when she reached her destination she would call them. Friday came, and Marie was admitted into the rehabilitation center. For thirty days, she made and received no phone calls as she struggled with the alcohol and cocaine withdrawals.

Meanwhile, Robert found employment at another security agency. A month went by, and there wasn't a day that he didn't think of Marie. He could hardly wait until she returned or called because he knew that she was the woman he wanted to marry and live with for the rest of his life.

Three months went by, but still there was no news of Marie. After six months of waiting and feeling sorry for himself, Robert decided to go out and find a new friend. Every night that he wasn't working, he would go downtown to the Torch Lounge and socialize. A lady walked in one night while Robert was sitting at the bar. At a glance Robert thought that she looked just like Marie. His first thought was to go to her, throw his arms around her, and tell her how much he had missed her. Then his pride got in the way. He thought, "If she cared for me, she should have called or gotten in touch somehow." He sat at the bar and drank his beer, wishing and hoping that she would recognize him and come over to the bar. That never happened because the lady he saw wasn't Marie. Robert left the bar and went home. While sitting home alone, Robert set his mind to forget about Marie.

Two more weeks went by. Then one evening the phone rang. "Hello Robert, this is Marie."

Robert said casually, "Well, how's it going for you these days?" "Oh, just fine since I've returned home."

"How was your trip?"

"About as well as it could have been," Marie replied. "Except, I did miss you very much, and I'm sorry for not keeping in touch. Can we meet somewhere and talk?"

"Let me check my itinerary," Robert said. He remained silent for a few seconds, and then said, "What time and where?"

Marie asked Robert to meet her at the same bar where they first met. Robert hesitated then said; "I'll see you Saturday at eight." He forgot about all the Heartache and pain that he felt while Marie was away. He forgot to tell her that he had set his mind to forget about her. Instead he decided to wait until Saturday.

When Marie hung up the phone, tears rushed down her cheeks. They were tears of joy and relief because, before she talked to Robert, she feared he wouldn't talk to her. She felt she could face Robert now because she was free from addiction. Marie had spent nearly seven months in rehab and received a certificate of rehabilitation. To her, it was as if she was on her way up. Now she was ready to commit. She would no longer be fearful of what falling in love would mean.

Marie arrived at the bar early. She was met with greetings from all of the familiar people that she knew. She was waiting and anticipating Robert's arrival. She sat in the same seat across the bar that she sat in when she first met him. Robert was at home pacing the floor. He was thinking of the way that Marie just disappeared, not calling or keeping in touch with him. For a long time he had longed to see and be with her, but she was nowhere to be found. He thought of the lonely days and nights that had passed since he had seen her face or heard her sweet voice. Now, at last, just as he had decided to put her out of his mind, she was back. He paced the floor, knowing that in a few moments he must decide whether or not to meet Marie at the bar. Then he began to think of excuses not to show up. He thought of reasons why he shouldn't go and reasons why he should. But Robert was one who would follow his heart, and it was his heart that convinced him that he should go to the bar and meet Marie. Deep down inside he knew that a relationship was what he really wanted from her. He loved her and wanted to marry her. He glanced at the clock and saw that there was just enough time left for him to make it to the bar by eight o'clock.

Not wasting any more time, he rushed out of the house, got into his car, and drove to the bar. When he arrived, he sat in his car for a few minutes trying to think of what he would say when he saw Marie. The thoughts that came were of how he had been missing her and wanting to see her for so long. Now that his loneliness was about to come to an end, he was nervous and wasn't thinking straight. Robert rubbed his forehead, got out of the car, and casually walked into the bar. He pretended not to notice that Marie was sitting on the other side of the bar in the same seat where she was sitting when they first met. Robert walked toward Marie, speaking to people sitting at the bar as he went.

As he approached Marie to greet her with a handshake, she looked into his eyes, and then brushed his hand away. She threw her arms around his neck, hugging him tightly. She whispered into his ear, "I've missed you so much."

Robert nervously responded, "I've missed you, too." They stared into each other's eyes for a few seconds, and then their lips touched. They stood there kissing as if there was no one else in the bar. Someone sitting at the bar cheered, and soon everyone began

To clap and laugh, giving the couple a standing ovation. Marie and Robert looked around the bar in a daze. They sat down and the crowd returned too normal. Robert said he wanted to talk to Marie about something important. They left the bar and went to a table.

"Well, tell me about your trip, since you didn't bother to keep in touch," Robert said.

"It's a long story," Marie started, "and I don't think this is the right time to discuss it. I will tell you that you were missed, and I was very lonely without you." "If you were so lonely, why didn't you

just pick up the phone and call me?" Marie remained silent. Then she tried to change the subject. "How have you been? Is there someone else in your life?"

"I've been doing fine, and I'm now employed with a security agency. There's no one else in my life at this time." Smiling, Robert said, "I don't know—maybe I shouldn't have told you about my feelings for you before you left. When I fell in love with you, it had been a very long time since I felt loved. The evening Phil introduced us at the bar I imagined that I'd be with you forever. I wanted to marry you and take you home with me. The first month that you were gone, I waited by the phone each night hoping you'd call. I even called your parents to see if they could tell me where you were, so I could come visit you."

Marie sat there with tears in her eyes, for she had the same feelings about Robert while she was a patient at the rehab center. She wanted to tell Robert where she had been and what had happened, but she feared that it might change his feelings toward her. She held his hands and said, "I'm sorry for all the loneliness and hurt I caused you, but believe me, I never intended to hurt you." She began to get up from the table, saying, "Well, I guess I'll say goodnight now."

"Wait," Robert said. "Are you leaving just like that?"

Marie threw her arms around Robert's neck, and while crying, she said, "I'm so sorry I hurt you. I never intended to do that. I've loved you and missed you so much since I've been away, and I didn't call you because I was afraid to."

Robert consoled her and then asked, "Are you ready to leave?" "Yes," said Marie, as Robert kissed her tears away.

"We'll take my car and come back for yours tomorrow," Robert decided. Marie was still teary-eyed and weak as she walked with Robert inside his house. He closed the door and began to kiss her, but Marie began to cry and asked if she could sit down.

"Sure," Robert said. "Right over here on the couch. Can I get you something to drink?"

"Yes," said Marie, with her voice trembling.

Robert went to the bar and got two glasses of wine. He handed one to Marie and sat beside her on the couch.

"I'm sorry," said Marie, "but I can't drink this." She passed the glass back to Robert. "I didn't tell you where I was going when I left because I didn't want you to think badly of me. I didn't even tell my family where I was going or when I was coming back." With tears in her eyes she said, "I used to use alcohol and drugs and until I met you I never realized that I needed help. I felt that I must get my problems cleared up.

"Oh," said Robert. "Is that what you meant when you said that before you commit to a relationship you must get something cleared up?"

"Yes," Marie said, glad to confess. "I felt that it was my problem, and I didn't want anyone else to get involved. I checked into the women's drug rehabilitation center."

"Are you rehabilitated now?" asked Robert.

"Yes, completely. Do you still feel the same about me?" Marie asked hopefully. Robert

leaned over and kissed her, saying, "Yes. I feel even closer to you than
Before now that I know why you left and didn't call. You couldn't imagine the thoughts that I was having when you left. I thought you had found someone else and decided to stay away. But now that you're back, please don't ever leave me again."

Robert stood up and took Marie by the hand. He led her to his bedroom while kissing her. He lifted her onto the bed and dimmed the lights. He took off her shoes, then her stockings. He stroked her legs with his hands. He lay beside her and kissed her forehead, her eyes, and her lips as he unbuttoned her dress. Then he pulled off his shirt and his pants.

He felt the soft smoothness of her body as he kissed her neck. He began to slip off her bra and kiss her stomach. He took one of her nipples in his mouth and sucked lightly on it. He licked her nipple with his tongue and blew it dry with his breath as he nibbled with his teeth. Marie moaned as she moved her body closer to his. Robert removed her panties and placed his hand between her legs, stroking her thighs. Her body began to squirm as he stroked. He placed his finger between the lips of her vagina, and Marie squeezed his hands with her thighs and moaned aloud as she reached an orgasm. Marie grabbed Robert's hand to remove it from between her legs. "I want you," she said, placing her hands on his genitals.

Robert got on top of her and entered her. Soon, they both screamed with pleasure. Robert kissed Marie and told her that he loved her. He remained on top of her, laid his head next to hers, and fell asleep. The next morning, they awoke and began kissing and caressing each other as if the night had never ended.

"Would you like me to get up and fix breakfast?" Marie eventually asked. "Yes," said Robert. "I'd like that very much."

Marie got up and went to the bathroom to wash up, then went to the kitchen to start breakfast. Later, Robert got up and went into the kitchen. Her back was turned, and she didn't see Robert when he entered. He stood in the doorway for a few minutes looking at Marie. She was dressed in one of his T-shirts, which showed the shape of her body. Standing there, he thought of how beautiful she looked and how good he felt making love to her. While her back was still turned, he walked up behind her, placed his hands on her shoulders, and began to kiss her on her neck and ears. She turned and, with her back against the counter, put her arms around his neck and kissed him. Their bodies came together hard, but slowly. Still kissing her, he began to stroke every inch of her body as she kissed him and moaned. Robert placed his hands on her buttocks, lifted her up, and placed her on the countertop with her legs spread. Marie moved her body forward. Robert let the towel that he had wrapped around him fall to the floor and placed his body between her legs. He entered her, and they moaned loudly as they reached a climax.

"We need to stop now," said Marie. "The bacon is burning." They quickly separated, and Marie rushed over to turn off the stove. After breakfast, she left Robert's house and went home to change clothes and get ready for work.

As time passed, they thought they could no longer stand to live apart. Robert came to the conclusion that he was going to ask Marie to marry him, but first he had to shop for a ring and find the proper time to propose.

One day after work, Robert went shopping for a ring, and he found one that he thought Marie would like. It was a nice, half-carat diamond with a slender gold band. Robert could hardly wait to ask her to marry him. On the weekend, Robert asked Marie out to dinner. He took her downtown to a restaurant and had called ahead to reserve a table for two, with candles and a beautiful view of the bay. When they arrived, they were met by the hostess and led to their table. "Oh, Robert," Marie exclaimed. "This is beautiful."

"I'm glad you like it," said Robert, "because I have something very important to ask you."

The waiter came over to the table and asked, "Are you ready to order or do you need more time?"

"Oh, I need more time," said Marie.

When the waiter left, Marie said, "What is it that you need to ask me?" Robert reached into his jacket pocket and pulled out a small black box. He opened
It and held it out in his hand. "Marie, I haven't known you for a very long time, but to me it seems as if I've known you all my life. I've fallen deeply in love with you, and I want you to be my wife. Will you marry me?" He passed the ring to Marie.

She hesitated a moment that could have been eternity. Then, with tears in her eyes, she said, "Yes, Robert, I'll marry you. The ring is so beautiful. I love it. I love you, too."

They ate without tasting their food, and gazed out the window to the bay without seeing anything but each other's reflection in the window. The next day they told their families, friends, and everyone at work about their decision to get married. Marie expressed to her girlfriends how romantic the mood was when Robert asked her to marry him. She described the entire scene, and they swooned at her story.

After about two weeks, Marie asked Robert about his suggestions for setting a date, time, and place for their wedding. He smiled at Marie and said, "Whenever and wherever you wish is fine with me, but I hope it's soon."

Marie replied, "How does July the fifteenth sound? We can have a night wedding."

"Sounds great," Robert said.

They decided on the church and where the reception would be held. Then her mother took over and made all the other plans, including the wedding rehearsals and bridal party. Within a month, all the plans were settled. Invitations were mailed out, and everything was set. Robert could hardly wait until the day would come for him to take Marie for his bride. In his quiet moments, he would sit and imagine how nice life was going to be for them.

Chapter 4

One evening after returning home from work, Marie received a phone call. A female on the other end said to Marie, "Don't marry Robert. He's mine. Leave him alone and find someone else." Then Marie heard a dial tone. Marie stood by the phone in astonishment. She had tried to recognize the voice, but she couldn't.

Later that evening, Robert came over to Marie's house for a visit. When he knocked on the door, Marie's first thought was to not let him in. She opened the door then turned away from him and walked into the dining room, barely sparing him a single glance. Robert walked behind Marie and placed his arms around her shoulders. He kissed her on the neck and asked, "What's wrong? Did you have a bad day at work?"

"No," said Marie, "but I need to talk with you about something. Sit down, and I'll fix you something to drink." Robert went into the living room and sat on the couch while Marie went to the

refrigerator and got a beer for him. She poured it into a glass and took it to the living room. She passed the glass to him and set next to him on the couch. She began to rub her forehead with her fingers, keeping silent. Her eyes began to fill with tears.

"You know, for a lady who is about to be married, you sure don't seem too happy," Robert said.

Marie took a deep breath and asked, "Robert, are you seeing someone else?" Robert had no idea what could have provoked such a question. He hesitated and Said, "Of course not. Why would you even ask that? Don't you trust me? Do you think I'd ask you to marry me if I was seeing someone else? Wait a minute. Are you having second thoughts about marrying me?"

"At first I didn't, but now I wonder," Marie said. "What brought this on?" Robert asked.

"Calm down," Marie said nervously. "This evening, when I got home from work, I got a call. The voice was female, and she said, 'don't marry Robert. Leave him alone. He's mine.' Then whoever it was hung up before I could get any information. I couldn't recognize the voice, and I didn't get the number on my caller ID because the call came from out of the area. That's why I asked you if you were seeing someone else. I thought maybe that person found out about our plans to get married and decided to call me." Marie began to sob and lowered her head.

Robert put his arms around her, and then he lifted her chin with his finger. He looked into her eyes and said, "I can't think of who would do such a thing. Surely no friend of mine would ever make a call like that, knowing the trouble it would cause. But I do know that I love you, and you're the only woman in my life. I could never cheat on you, and the thought of cheating never even crossed my mind, not even when we were apart. As far as the phone call, it was probably from someone who's jealous of our decision to get married and wanted to see if they could cause problems for us. I hope you don't let this come between us."

Marie said, "I love you very much. This one incident can't change the way I feel about you. I want to marry you, but please don't hurt me. I've been hurt so many times in past relationships I don't think I could stand to be hurt anymore," Marie sobbed.

"Don't cry," said Robert. "There's no reason to despair. I'm here for you, and I'll always be here for you whenever you need me. I love you." He took a long swallow of his beer and settle back on the couch to watch TV. Holding tightly to Robert, Marie began to imagine their marriage and nearly forgot about the upsetting phone call.

While watching TV until late at night, they fell asleep on the couch and slept through the night. When morning came, Robert opened his eyes and heard the TV still on. Marie had fallen asleep with her head on his shoulder. He looked at the clock hanging on the wall, which read seven thirty. He saw daylight and realized they had overslept. Robert shook Marie and called out her name. "Marie, you're going to be late for work."

Marie woke from dreaming about married life with Robert. In her dream, she had gotten dressed and ready for work. Robert drove her to work because he was going to use their one car. While Marie was at work, she began to get suspicious of Robert. In the confusing way dreams often go, she was thinking, *why did he drive me to work? He has his own car, and I have mine. Maybe he didn't want me to know what he was going to do today.* In her dream, Marie borrowed a friend's car and drove home. She saw two cars parked in the driveway. One was hers, but she didn't recognize the other one. Robert had given her the impression that he was going to work after he dropped her off at her job. She thought maybe something had gone wrong.

She parked down the street and walked up to the porch. She went around the side of the house to the bedroom window. As she came closer she heard music playing loudly. Through the window, she saw Robert and a woman. They had no clothes on. Robert was sitting in an easy chair across from the bed, and the woman was kneeling between his legs. Marie saw the woman's head moving up and down and from side to side. She watched in shock as Robert leaned back in the chair, crying out with pleasure. Marie tried to knock on the window and yell to Robert to let him know that she was looking at him, but it seemed as if he couldn't hear her.

Robert lifted the woman up and placed her in the bed. He kissed her on the lips and then all over her body. With his head at the foot of the bed and her head at the top of the bed, they began to kiss each other's bodies. Marie watched as Robert put his head between the woman's legs, and the woman put her head between Robert's legs and they began to moan and rock from side to side. In Marie's dream there was nothing she could do but look. She continued to watch as Robert and the woman reached a climax.

Robert began shaking Marie again. She jumped up from the couch and said, "Oh my God." She threw her arms around Robert and squeezed him as she said, "I was dreaming an awful dream."

"What did you dream?" Robert asked. "I…I'll tell you about it later."

Robert looked at the clock, and realizing what time it was, kissed Marie, told her good-bye, and rushed out the door. Marie watched as he rushed to his car. "I'll call you later," Robert said, and he drove away.

Marie tried not to think about the upsetting phone call that she had received the day before. She tried very hard to push it out of her mind, but she couldn't forget it. That thought, and the images from the dream, weighed heavily on her mind. She started to wonder what he was doing whenever he wasn't with her. Marie went so far as to have one of her friends call Robert at work while she was on the other line so she could hear his voice when he answered. When he said hello, Marie's friend said she had dialed a wrong number and hung up. Marie listened to Robert's voice from the other line and was sure that he was at work. Even so, as Marie's wedding day came near, she grew more and more suspicious of Robert. At times she would refuse dates with him, then drive to his house and follow him around in her car to see if he was being unfaithful. When Robert would come over to visit her, Marie would give him the silent treatment, as if he had done something wrong.

One evening Robert called from work and asked Marie to go out with him. She said, "Are you sure your other friend won't mind?"

He acted as if he didn't hear her and said, "I'll pick you up at eight o'clock." "Okay," Marie said doubtfully. "I think I'll be ready when you get here." Robert went home, got dressed, and gave Marie a call, but there was no answer. He called again, but still there was no answer. He drove over to Marie's house. When he arrived he knocked on the door, but there was no answer. He walked back to his car and waited for a while, trying to think of what might have happened to her. Robert sat in the car for about a half hour before deciding to go back home and see if Marie tried to get in touch with him or left a message.

Inside the house, Marie had reached the point at which she couldn't deal with her suspicious thoughts. She was sure that he was doing something wrong, even without any evidence or reason. *That's what men are like*, she thought. She paced the floor thinking about what to do next. The

thought of a drink was on her mind until finally she thought one drink wouldn't hurt. When she saw through the window that Robert had left, she went to the bar for a drink.

When Robert arrived home, there was no message on his answering machine. He called Marie again and left a message. He was worried but didn't know what else to do. Eventually he fell asleep on the couch next to the phone.

Marie sat at the bar. One drink didn't seem to do anything, so she had another, then another, eventually losing track of time. Soon she hardly knew what she was doing. She was leaning on the barstool, mostly upright, when a guy approached her. "Is this seat taken?" he asked.

Marie looked at him blurrily. At first glance she thought the guy was Robert. She said, "It's about time you got here, Robert. What took you so long? Were you out with your other woman?" Then she smiled and laughed.

"No," the guy said with a grin. "I fell asleep, and when I woke up, I knew I needed to come pick you up and take you home. Are you ready, dear?"

Marie stood up and staggered out of the bar. The guy followed her to her car. Marie rubbed her forehead and turned around. She looked at him carefully. It wasn't Robert. "Who are you?" she asked.

"I'm Robert, don't you remember?" "Robert who?" Marie asked.

"I don't know. You called me Robert, so I'm the Robert you want me to be," the guy said.

**"I don't know you. What are you doing here?" Marie asked still hazy. The guy walked back toward the bar saying, "That's okay. I don't know you
Either, but you'll be fine in the morning."**

Marie got into her car and drove home. She started undressing immediately inside the doorway and headed straight to the bathroom. Under cold shower water, she thought of what she had done. She was disappointed in herself; especially with the way she had treated Robert. She knew she should call him and explain, but fearful of what he might say, she couldn't find the courage to call him. She certainly didn't want to talk to him half-drunk. Marie went to bed telling herself she would be all right in the morning.

Robert got up around six o'clock. It had been a rough night for him. He stayed awake most of the night thinking of Marie and wondering why she didn't call. He paced the floor, trying to decide whether or not to get in touch with Marie before work. He was concerned about her because unless there was something wrong, he knew she would have called him. He thought. "*Maybe she had an accident of some kind and had gone to the hospital. Still, she could have called from the hospital,* he thought. No matter how he tried to excuse the fact that Marie didn't call him, he could not think of a reason that sounded reasonable. He finally decided to call Marie before going to work.

Her phone rang, but again there was no answer. After listening to the phone ring and ring, he got dressed and went to work. At break time, he went to a pay phone on the job site. This time he called Marie at her office. They told him that she didn't come to work that day. Negative thoughts about her roiled through his mind, predominant among them the feeling that she was avoiding him.

He became more depressed as the day went on, and his thoughts grew angry. He was

wondering if this was the way it was going to be when they were married. *If so,* he thought, *then maybe we should just call the wedding off.* In spite of his negative thoughts, Robert called her at home. After the phone rang about six times, Marie picked up the phone.

"Hello?" she answered.

"This is Robert. Did I wake you up?"

"Yes, but it's okay," Marie said. Her voice was dry and drowsy. "I've been trying to get in touch with you since yesterday," Robert said,
Concerned. "What happened? Where were you? Did you forget that we had a date set for last night?"

"No, I didn't forget about our date, but right now my stomach is upset, and I don't feel like explaining anything to you over the phone. Can we talk this evening? I need to take something to help my stomach."

"Well," said Robert, "I have to return to work anyway. But I'll be by your house at eight tonight, and we'll discuss this further."

"Okay," Marie said miserably.

Robert felt relieved to hear Marie's voice, but that didn't prevent the thoughts he was having about their relationship.

Marie was at home trying to do her household chores, but she couldn't keep her mind on them because she was thinking of what had happened to her last night. How was she going to tell Robert? She was worried about what he would think and how he would react when she told him. She felt ashamed of herself for the way she had behaved, but she excused her actions by thinking that Robert was probably seeing someone else. She thought that if he could do it, then she could screw up at least once and get away with it. That kind of thinking helped a little, but she still had to find the courage to face Robert that evening. The closer it got to the time for Robert to come over, the more depressed Marie became. Her stomach was in knots. She lay down in bed and tried to rest.

When Robert got home from work, he dialed her number, and when she answered, he said, "Hello, I'll be over as soon as I can take a shower and put on some clothes."

Marie was silent for a moment before saying, "I don't think I would be very good company for you this evening. I'm not feeling well."

"Then I'll come over and sit with you," Robert suggested.

"Thanks, but I think I need to lie in my bed and rest. I'm sure I'll feel better in the morning."

Robert replied, "Okay. I hope you get better, and I'll talk to you tomorrow. Call me if you need anything." They said good-bye and hung up.

Now Robert was almost certain that Marie was avoiding him purposefully. He felt that he was being left out of her life, and she was letting him down easy. He began to doubt continuing their relationship and started thinking of what he would do without Marie. He knew from previous

experience that if he and Marie broke up it would take time for him to get over her, and during that time there would be heartaches and pain. For now, he decided, he would play it by ear.

Marie laid on her bed trying to get over her upset stomach and still trying to find courage enough to face Robert and tell him what had happened to her. She started several times to call him, but she kept changing her mind for fear of what he might think of her and what he might say. She wanted to tell him in the right way because she was afraid to cause problems with their plans for marriage.

Marie grew tired of the frustration and once again she decided to go out for a drink. She thought by drinking she wouldn't feel so bottled up inside, and it would help ease her stomach ache. She got up, put on her clothes, and went to the bar. She took a seat and ordered a drink. She sat there thinking and wondering about her relationship with Robert. After enough drinks, her attitude began to grow uncaring.

"I'm going to just tell him what happened, and if he doesn't like it we can just break up," she mumbled to herself walking out of the bar. Marie drove home, walked directly to the bathroom, and vomited. Afterward, she went to her bedroom, and passed out on the bed.

Chapter 5

Robert woke up the next day still having doubts about his relationship. He wanted to call Marie but it was too early, so he got dressed and went to work. While at work, he decided not to get in touch with Marie until the workday was over. He thought that he needed more time to speak with her than the job would allow. In the past few days, Robert had worried so much about Marie that he could hardly wait until the end of the workday to be with her and talk to her. Today, however, he thought he would get some yard work done before calling her.

That day, Marie went to the doctor to get something for her stomachache. After examining her, the doctor told her that she was pregnant.

"Are you sure?" Marie asked.

"Just as sure as I'm standing here," the doctor said.

Marie didn't know whether to be upset or excited. But she did know that she had to talk to Robert about it. When she got home she waited anxiously for Robert to come over, so she could tell him that she was pregnant. As the time grew nearer she could hold out no longer. When she thought he had left work and was at home, she dialed Robert's number, but the only voice she heard was the answering machine saying that Robert was unable to answer the phone. The message on the machine asked Marie to leave her name and number at the sound of the beep, but because she was suspicious regarding the reason why Robert didn't answer the phone. She left no message. Marie's phone rang a few moments later. When she answered, she heard Robert's voice.

"Did you call?" he asked.

"Yes," Marie replied. "I just called to let you know that I'm making dinner for us this evening."

"Oh good," Robert said. "I'm starving. Is there anything special that I can bring?" "No," said Marie, "just bring yourself."

"Okay, I'll be there soon."

"I need to check on the food. I'll talk to you when you get here," Marie said. Robert said good-bye and hung up. It was a rushed day for Marie, for she had reintroduced her body to alcohol and had to deal with the after-effects. But she was sure that she could make it through the evening.

Robert arrived and knocked on the door. When Marie opened the door, their eyes met. Marie felt somewhat ashamed and held her head down as she said hello.

"What's this? Aren't you glad to see me? Don't I get a kiss or a hug anymore?" he asked smiling.

Marie blushed and then smiled. She gave Robert a kiss and a hug. She asked him to come in, sit down, and make himself comfortable while she got dinner ready.

Robert sat on the couch in the living room, and Marie asked if she could bring him something to drink.

"Yes," said Robert, as he reached for the remote control. Marie went into the kitchen and poured a glass of soda and brought it to Robert.

"Dinner will be ready in a little while," she said. Then she went back into the kitchen. For dinner, she had prepared rib eye steak with green beans, mashed potatoes, sweet rolls, and green salad. Once the table was set, she went into the living room and told Robert that dinner was ready.

"Okay," Robert said, and he went into the bathroom to wash his hands. He came in and sat down at the table.

After dinner Robert complimented Marie on a delicious meal. "I'll be finished cleaning the kitchen in just a bit," Marie said. She went into the kitchen, and Robert went into the living room, sat down on the couch, and turned on the TV. While Marie cleaned the kitchen, she thought of what she was going to say to Robert. She was worried about how he would feel, what he would think, and what his response would be. She wanted to just come out and tell him the truth about what happened to her the other night, and about being pregnant, but she didn't have the courage. She poured a couple of glasses of scotch and drank them down quickly. Robert got up and went to the kitchen door. Marie was standing at the sink. He stood at the door for a few seconds, admiring Marie from behind.

"Are you sure I can't help you with the dishes?"

Startled, Marie answered, "Oh no, I can handle it. I'll be finished in just a few more minutes. You just sit back and relax." Robert smiled and returned to the living room. Marie, still not thinking of the danger that she might be doing to her child, took a few more sips of scotch. She poured a glass of wine for Robert and went into the living room.

"Thank you," said Robert, raising his glass and sipping the wine. Then Marie questioned Robert about his day at work.

"Well, I guess you could say the day went by quickly, considering the fact that I tried to rush it, wishing that it was over, so it would be closer to the time to come visit you. After all, I haven't seen you in a few days, and I was beginning to worry. I came by your house the other night when I couldn't reach you. I thought something had happened to you. I didn't know what to do or think since I wasn't able to get in touch with you. What happened to you that night?"

"Well," Marie started, "I'm going to be up front with you, especially since we're about to be married. I was having doubts about our relationship. I had begun to think you were seeing someone else besides me. I even went so far as to call your job to see if you were really at work. I didn't confront you about it because I didn't want you to feel that I didn't trust you, and I didn't want you to think that I was being possessive. I became depressed and upset. So, trying to handle the depression that evening when you were supposed to pick me up, I decided to go down to the bar and have a drink, in hopes that the drink would help me to cope. My intention was to return before you got to my house but after a few drinks, I lost track of time. I ended up drinking all night long. The next day I was sick. The day after that I felt ashamed of what I'd done, so ashamed that I didn't have the courage to face you and tell you about it. Now I'm telling you, and I'm sorry for what happened."

Before Marie could tell Robert about her being pregnant, he shouted at her, "How could you? How could you jeopardize our future and all the time it took to rehabilitate you? What were you thinking? You are going to have to make a decision. Either you stop drinking, or we're going to have to call it quits. Which is it going to be?"

Marie opened her mouth as if to speak, but instead she placed her hands over her face and began to cry. Robert got up from the couch and walked toward the door. In anger he said, "Since you can't give me an answer, call me when you can." And he walked out the door, slamming it behind him.

Marie sat there on the couch and cried. She was somewhat relieved that she had told Robert what happened to her the other night, but she didn't get the chance to tell him about her pregnancy. She was hurt at the way he responded. Now she was beginning to feel that she was losing her way, and as she sat crying, she thought about the things Robert had said to her before he left. She thought about her condition before she fell in love with Robert and how she had to check herself into the rehabilitation center. *It's true,* she thought. *If I keep drinking when I'm confused in order to cope with my problems, I will end up in the hospital or the rehab center for sure.* Out loud she said, "That's not going to happen to me." She rubbed her stomach and said, "That's not going to happen to *us.*"

Driving home, Robert was upset and he decided to stop at the bar for a drink. After a few drinks, he thought about what he had said to Marie and how he had said it. He began to question if he had done the right thing. He finally made the decision that he could have handled the situation better. At once he stopped drinking. When he tried to get up from the bar, he sat back down. He realized that he drank a little too much. After taking deep breaths to revive himself he got up, hurried to the pay phone and dialed Marie's number.

"Hello?" she answered.

"I'm sorry for saying those things and leaving the way I did. I was upset and angry, and I couldn't stand the thought of you having to go away to be rehabilitated again. I hope you can find it in your heart to forgive me."

"I forgive you," Marie said, "and you were right about the drinking. But just because I had a couple of drinks that time doesn't mean I'm going to continue. We agreed that if there came a time when we felt different about things, we'd sit down and discuss it, but when I told you the truth, you got up and walked out on me before I could get myself together, to try to make you understand why I did what I did. You don't know how bad that hurt me, and all I could do was cry myself to sleep. But that's okay, I'm a big girl, and I can handle that. But sometimes I'm not so strong." She began to cry again as she said, "I'm human, and I make mistakes just like anyone else. And besides

that, I'm pregnant." Then she hung up.

Robert didn't believe what he had just heard, but he shouted, "I'm going to be a father!" He called again, and Marie answered. "Marie, please don't hang up on me," Robert begged. "I'm sorry for making you feel bad. I'm sorry for everything that I said. Can I come over and talk so we can try to work this out? I promise not to stay long."

"Okay," Marie agreed.

"I'll be there in just a few minutes."

Minutes later, Robert walked back through her door and held out his hand. Marie placed her hand in his and stood up. He put his arms around her and looked into her eyes and said, "I'm sorry."

Marie couldn't hold back the tears. She threw both arms around his neck as she cried and said, "I love you, and I don't want to lose you. I want to marry you, and I know I can be a good wife. I want us to raise our child together."

"I know, baby," Robert said, as he kissed the tears from her eyes. "Don't cry. Everything's going to be all right. I'm going to be here for you no matter what." They sat on the couch silently, with their heads together.

As the days passed, Marie thought about how Robert had walked out on her when she needed him most. She thought, *What if we were married and had an argument? Would he just walk out on his child and me and leave us to make it on our own? This is his entire fault.* Although Marie still cared about their relationship, things just didn't feel the same after so much suspicions and disappointment.

Realizing that Marie was changing, Robert felt poorly. One day after work he decided to stop at the bar to have a drink or two before going home. He sat drinking and thinking until well after seven o'clock. Normally, he would have called Marie sooner to ask her how she was feeling and to find out if there was anything he could do or get for her.

Robert had several drinks and lost track of time, and he didn't call Marie. He excused himself by thinking Marie didn't want to be bothered with him anyway. He took another drink and stayed at the bar. Robert had not made love with Marie for a while. He was painfully aware that he was longing for affection. A woman walked in and sat in the seat next to him. She had long black hair and blue eyes, and she wore a tight, red mini skirt.

Robert needed someone to talk to so he introduced himself. "May I get you something to drink? What will you have?"

"My name's Nancy. I'll have a vodka tonic, thanks," she replied. Robert called the bartender over and ordered drinks for them. As Robert and Nancy sat at the bar drinking, they began talking. After a few drinks, they were feeling comfortable with each other and started to talk about some of their personal problems. Robert began talking about Marie, and Nancy began to tell Robert about her friend, Richard. They found out they had similar problems. They talked and drank until midnight and then went their separate ways.

Every day for about two weeks Robert would get off work and call Marie to ask how she was

doing, but they had little else to say to each other. Robert became bored, so he would change clothes after work and go to the bar. Nancy would be there when he arrived, or sometimes she would get there first. But each time they met, they would greet each other with a smile, sit next to each other, and begin drinking and talking. Robert started seeing more of Nancy than he did of Marie. The more Nancy and Robert talked, the more they liked each other, and the closer they became. Robert told her that he was getting married in about a week and about the problems he was having with Marie.

Nancy said, "Robert, I like you, and I think being friends with you is great. We've become close, but you need to promise me something."

"Okay," said Robert. "What is it?"

"You need to promise me that you won't ask me to give you my opinion about Marie, and I won't ask you for an opinion about my man. This way, it'll eliminate a lot of harsh feelings between us."

"Fine," said Robert. When they got ready to leave that night, they put their arms around each other to hold the other up as they walked out of the bar to their cars.

Richard was Nancy's friend and lover. One night while Robert and Nancy were leaving the bar with their arms around each other, Richard's best friend, Larry, saw them. He had been sitting in the bar drinking and noticed them as they left. All Larry could think was that Nancy was cheating on Richard. Larry and Richard were employed with the same company, and they had lunch together almost every day. The next day at lunch, Larry asked Richard if he and Nancy were on good terms.

"Yes," Richard said, "but it's just like any other relationship. Sometimes we're up, and sometimes we're down, you know."

"Richard, you know I'm your friend, and you know I wouldn't lie to you, don't You?"

"Yeah," replied Richard, "what are you trying to say?" "Okay," Larry started. "First, promise me you won't get offended." "Okay," Richard said, "I won't. So tell me."

"Well, last night I went down to the bar for a few drinks, and I saw Nancy sitting at the bar with this guy."

"So?" Richard said. "Nancy goes to the bar for drinks occasionally. I don't expect her to sit at home like a knot on a log."

"Well, the guy put his arms around her, and they left together." "What does that mean? Why are you telling me this?" Richard asked.

"Because you're my friend, and I don't like seeing my friends being cheated," Larry said.

Richard never said anything to Nancy about what Larry had told him because Richard and Nancy had an agreement that if either of them ever felt that they wanted to see someone else, they

would let the other know about it. But the thought of what Larry had told him weighed heavily on his mind.

That night Richard decided to follow Nancy as she went to the bar. He sat in his car in the parking lot as Nancy walked into the bar. Richard waited to see her leave and with whom she was leaving. As usual, Robert and Nancy sat at the bar drinking. Richard watched. At midnight, Robert walked Nancy to her car with his arms around her. Richard saw them. When Nancy opened her car door, she dropped her keys. Robert told Nancy to go ahead and get into the car, and he would get her keys for her. He bent over and picked up the keys, leaned over, and handed them to her through the window. Then Nancy drove away.

Richard followed Nancy home that night. He thought about what he had seen, Nancy hugging Robert as they left the bar. He thought about how Robert leaned over after letting Nancy into her car, probably kissing her. Although Richard was upset about what he thought he saw, he managed to remain calm. He was on probation and couldn't afford to get into any trouble.

After he saw that Nancy had gone into her apartment, he sat in his car waiting to see if Robert would come over. Robert never showed up. Before morning, Richard went home so Nancy wouldn't know that he had been spying on her. At work that day, Richard thought it all over. He decided to find out about Robert, to see if he had a girlfriend or a wife. Richard's plan was to expose Robert to his wife or girlfriend as a cheater.

Richard went to the bar early during the day. He inquired about Robert. The bartender knew Robert and knew he was getting married because Robert had given him an invitation. The bartender even told Richard who Robert was marrying and where Marie lived. With this information, Richard began to think about different ways to expose Robert. At first he thought about calling Marie and asking her on a date. He thought that might take too long though. Some women didn't go out the first time they met someone. Then he thought of writing her a letter, accusing Robert of seeing his girlfriend on the side. Richard thought that wouldn't work either. He decided to call her up and tell her what was going on and see what she said.

That evening, just after she had finished talking to Robert, Marie's phone rang. She answered, and at first no one said anything. Just when Marie was about to hang up, a voice said, "Your soon to-be husband is cheating on you with my girlfriend. I don't have time to go into details, but if you want to see for yourself, you can see them at Mike's Bar at eight o'clock."

The caller hung up. Marie had noticed that when Robert called, he didn't have much to say anymore. *Could it be that he found someone else he likes better than me?* She thought. *Is he really the kind of guy that would cheat before his wedding or is he planning not to marry me? If Robert wasn't seeing anyone else, then why didn't he tell me that he was going to the bar tonight?*

Marie decided to go to Mike's at eight o'clock. When she arrived, she saw Robert's car. She decided against going into the bar because she didn't have the courage to confront him. She parked in the lot across the street, in a place where she could see

Robert when he left. At about midnight, Marie saw Robert and a woman leave the bar. They had their arms around each other as Robert walked her to her car. He opened the door for her, let her in, and leaning over in the window, said goodnight. She drove away, but from where Marie was sitting, it looked as if he leaned into the window and kissed the woman before she left.

Robert then went to his car and drove away. Marie didn't say anything to Robert about what she had seen for fear of ruining the wedding that was just a few days away. Marie put off seeing Robert the week of the wedding. She thought that if she didn't see him, she would be able to handle what she had seen.

Chapter 6

At the wedding shower, Marie tried very hard to hide her unhappiness, but she couldn't hide it from her mother. Her mother knew that she was unhappy, but she dropped the subject when Marie said she didn't want to discuss it. Only days before her wedding day, Marie found it easier not to think of the incident at the bar. Marie knew that whenever she would come face-to-face with Robert, she couldn't look him in the eye because if she did, she would burst into tears. Each night Marie cried and prayed for the courage to go through with the wedding, not just for her sake, but for her child's sake as well. Robert was the father of her child, and although she had doubts about marrying him, she set them aside because she didn't want her child to be born out of wedlock.

Marie and Robert followed the traditional prohibition against the groom seeing the bride the night before their wedding day. That night Robert was invited out for a few drinks with his nephew to celebrate the occasion. The more they drank, the more Robert wanted to see Marie. When Robert would make an attempt to call her, his nephew and friends would stop him. "We're going to have to keep an eye on you. You know you're not supposed to see the bride before tomorrow. You're trying to rush it," they said and laughed. Then they took him by the arm and guided him from club to club. The idea was to keep Robert busy so he couldn't visit Marie until the next day. They kept Robert out partying until three o'clock in the morning. He was too intoxicated to drive himself home, so he slept at his nephew's house.

Marie worried because she had tried to call Robert at his house early in the morning, but she hadn't been able to get in touch with him. She called his nephew's house. "Have you seen Robert?"

"Oh sure," said his nephew, "he's here asleep on the couch. He had a rough night, so I brought him home with me. Hold on, I'll wake him up."

"Oh, no. Let him rest for now, but make sure he's at the church on time for the wedding."

Robert woke up at twelve-thirty. As he got up from the couch, he said, "There are things I have to do before the wedding." Robert had made plans to get dressed at his future brother-in-law's house, and then go to the church from there. Robert's nephew lived forty minutes away from Robert's brother-in-law's house, and an hour away from Robert's house. Robert feared that if he didn't leave right away, he would be late for his own wedding. He said good-bye to his nephew and family, got into his car, and drove

Away. It took him an hour to get home. He felt relieved as he began to gather his things together, getting ready to go over to his brother-in-law's to get dressed.

When he finished it was two o'clock. The wedding wasn't until five thirty that evening, so Robert thought there was plenty of time for him to relax a little before he left. He lay back on the couch and watched TV until he fell asleep. He woke at three thirty, and he still had to drive forty minutes to reach Marie's brother's house. He had to be at the church at five o'clock. Robert gathered up his things and his tuxedo and rushed to his car. He drove well over the speed limit. When he arrived, it was four o'clock. He rushed inside the house and everyone was glad to see him.

"How's everyone doing?" Robert asked. "Where do I get dressed? I don't want to be late."

Robert's brother-in-law showed him to the dressing room. By the time he got dressed, it was four-thirty. Robert still had to drop his car off at the reception hall so that he and Marie would have transportation after the reception. Robert asked one of the guys in the wedding party to follow him over to the reception hall, and then give him a ride to the church.

Everyone was gathered at the church but the bride and the groom. When Robert arrived, the bride had not made it there yet. She and the bridal party soon arrived on a private trolley, and the wedding started.

It was a beautiful ceremony. All the bridesmaids were dressed in fuchsia gowns. The groomsmen wore white tuxedos trimmed in fuchsia, and the groom wore all white. Marie and Robert rushed out of the church, greeting their friends as they left. They got on the trolley and rode to the reception hall.

When the wedding party entered the hall along with Robert and Marie, an aisle was made for them and the guests stood and applauded. After the announcement of the bride and groom's party, they started to mingle. Robert tried to get together with Marie, but she seemed to ignore him, so he excused himself and went to the front of the building to have a cigarette. Robert was surprised that Marie had been looking for him. Marie grabbed Robert's hand and coaxed him to the table for food.

Robert sat at the head table and ate while Marie made her way off to her friends and relatives. He thought this was the story of his life. *Here I am at my own wedding reception, with a crowd of people around me, and I still feel lonely.* Robert made it through the reception as he watched Marie do everything within her power to stay away from him. That night, when the reception was over, Robert wanted to be alone with his wife. Instead he was asked to attend a get-together party at the local bar with Marie and some of her friends. Robert was tired and wanted to go home, but he knew that Marie wasn't ready, so they both went to the bar. By the time they got home, they were too tired to make love, so they got in bed and went to sleep.

As the days went by Marie would come home from work with a look of anger and disgust on her face. She would eat her dinner and then sit at the table, pretending to read the newspaper. When Robert tried to start a conversation with her, she would snap angrily at him. There would be no communication for the rest of the night.

One day when she snapped at Robert, he asked her, "Are you happy living here with me?"

She answered in a dull voice, "I guess it'll do."

Robert asked her if there was something wrong, and she replied, "No, there's nothing wrong."

When they would go out, Marie would act as if she didn't want to be with Robert and didn't want to talk to him. Her actions began to become embarrassing to Robert. He didn't feel good about being with Marie in public. They quarreled often about everything.

One day Robert said angrily, "We can't even communicate, so why are we even together?"

"Fine," said Marie, "I'll just leave."

Marie grabbed the telephone and called her mother to ask if her room was still available. Her mother told her it was.

"I'll leave right now," Marie said, as she gathered up her clothes. When Robert realized that Marie was about to leave, he walked over to her and said,
"Please, don't leave me. I'm sorry I upset you. I just want us to talk more." He kissed her and asked her to stay.

"All right, I'll stay, but the next time you say something like that to me, I'm leaving you," she warned.

Two weeks went by, and Marie was following her same routine. Robert had begun to feel that he could do better by himself instead of sitting around while his wife ignored him. They got into a quarrel, and Robert said, "I want a divorce because this isn't working. We have differences that seem unsolvable. We don't need to be together."

"Well, I'm leaving then," Marie, stated.

Marie called her mother and began packing her things. Robert sat quietly in the other room. He regretted that Marie was leaving him, and he wished that there was something he could do or say to make her stay, but deep down inside, he knew if he asked her to stay, it would only cause an argument, and things would be the same. Hurting inside, he sat quietly as she walked out of the room and left. A feeling of gloom came over him. He really loved Marie, but he just couldn't deal with her actions.

A few days passed. Robert decided to see a lawyer to request an uncontested divorce. The lawyer told Robert the procedures and said that he and Marie would have to be present to sign papers. When Robert got home, he called Marie. "Hello. May I speak to Marie?" he asked.

When Marie came to the phone, Robert hesitated for a moment. Then he told her that he had gone to a lawyer and requested information on a divorce. He told her that they would have to sign papers in order to get an uncontested divorce. When Marie began to cry, Robert was surprised. "Isn't this what you want?" he asked. "Isn't that what you told me before you left me?"

"Yes," said Marie, "but I was angry then. I don't want to divorce you. I love you." Robert didn't know what to say. Considering what had happened between them and how torn apart he had been when Marie left him, he was fascinated that she still loved him. It also made him angry. He thought of all the other times that he had begged her not to leave him but she did anyway. Now that he had made up his mind to do something about it, she said she didn't want the divorce.

"Well," said Robert, "I want a divorce. I've applied for it, and I'll pay for it. All you need to do is sign it like you said you'd do before you walked out on me. I'd appreciate it if you'd find the time to sign the decree when you get it and then mail it back to the lawyer's office as soon as possible. In sixty days, you and I will be finished

Legally." Robert was so angry with Marie that he hung up on her and headed to the bar for a well-deserved drink. He and the owner were the last to leave.

For a few days Robert did some serious thinking about his situation. He knew that even though he and Marie weren't together, he still longed to be with her. When his telephone would

ring, he would have to control himself to keep from rushing to answer it because he thought it might be Marie calling. He was disappointed when it wasn't her. Robert set his mind to the reality that he was going to be divorced, and he must get over the hurt that it was going to cause him. He had put it into his mind that things happen but life still goes on, and so would he.

As for Marie, once again, despair hung over her head. She called Robert's house day after day but there was no answer. She began to fear that if she signed the divorce papers, she would lose Robert for sure. She thought of drinking to help her cope with her problems, but when she thought of the child inside of her, she changed her mind. Her family began to think that Marie's choice to marry Robert was wrong. Marie wished that she had told Robert that she saw him with another woman instead of holding it inside, using it to spite him every chance she got. She knew that she had only acted the way she did because she couldn't get the thought out of her mind that he was with someone else.

Marie decided to suspend the divorce and seek counseling instead. She talked to her minister and told him what had happened. She asked if he would act as mediator between her and Robert. Her minister called Robert and invited him to dinner in order to talk his problems out.

Robert met with the minister, and after a long talk about his and Marie's marriage, Robert decided that his mind was made up and no one could change it. The minister then asked Robert if he would call Marie as a favor to him and let her know that he had talked to him about their problem.

"I'll do that," Robert said, as he got up from the table. Robert thanked the minister for the dinner, shook hands, and said good-bye.

Even though Robert had told the minister that he would call Marie, he was still having second thoughts about his decision. As long as he didn't talk to her or see her, the pain of being without her didn't surface regularly. But Robert was a man of his word. He had given his word to a man of God, and he wasn't going to break it. That evening he called Marie.

When she answered, Robert said, "I talked to your minister, and he told me of your feelings. I told him I'd call you and let you know that I talked to him, but talking to him didn't change anything. I still want the divorce."

Marie began to cry as she said, "I'm not giving you a divorce. If you didn't want me, you shouldn't have married me. You're in my life now, and I want to keep you there. What about all the plans we made for our child and us? Don't you care to stick around and make them come true? What about our child? Do you want him to grow up without his father? How can you say that you want a divorce when you know that it will cause your child and me to suffer? Did you ever really love me or were you just waiting for the opportunity to find a reason to divorce me so you could be with that other woman? It's not going to work!" She hung up the phone.

Robert didn't know what to think. Since he had already paid for the divorce, he decided to let things stay as they were and continue with his divorce for now.

A few weeks passed, and Robert felt love-starved and lonely. At night, when he tried to sleep, he would think of Marie and how he felt about her before they got married. He had never thought that their marriage would end up like this. He had always thought that their love would last forever. In despair, he would stop at the bar after work to try to forget his problems. Although he

felt better for a little while when he drank, the problems were still there when he stopped drinking. He thought maybe the child would be better off without him and Marie being together because their quarreling would have caused the child more problems.

One evening when Robert stopped at the bar, his friend Nancy was sitting there having a drink. He went to the seat next to her and asked, "Is anyone sitting here?"

Nancy started to say yes, but when she realized it was Robert, she smiled and laughed. "Hey Robert, how are you?"

"Long time, no see," Robert said with a smile. He called the bartender over and ordered drinks for the both of them. After a few drinks, Robert began to try to find out if Nancy was seeing anyone.

"Why don't you just come right out and ask if I'm still seeing Richard," Nancy laughed. "We know each other well enough for you to do that. We're still friends, aren't we?"

"Yeah," said Robert.

"Then you know you don't have to beat around the bush with me about anything," Nancy stated.

"Okay. How is it with you and Richard?"

"Well," said Nancy as she drank, "it's a long story, believe me. But if you have the time to listen, I'll tell you about it."

"Sure," Robert said.

"Okay, here it is. I caught Richard in bed with another woman. She jumped up, put on her clothes, and ran out of my apartment before I could get my hands on her. I asked him, 'What is the meaning of this?' He said that the other woman didn't mean anything to him, and he wouldn't see her again. He told me he only had the other woman because he thought that I was cheating on him with you when we used to hang out drinking together. I thought about it, and maybe he did think that I was seeing you because, after all, we were drinking every night together. So I forgave him.

"After a few weeks, I noticed he started being too tired to make love to me when he came over. He said he wasn't feeling well and that he'd probably have to see a doctor. I guess he forgot that I had a key to his apartment, or he didn't care. But after talking to him on the phone, I felt bad about him being sick, so I decided to go over to his apartment and sit with him.

"When I got there, I didn't knock very hard because I thought I might wake him up. I put the key in the door, opened it, and walked in. I didn't see Richard in the living room so, on the way to the bedroom, I called out for him softly. I put my hand on the doorknob, and when I opened the door, Richard was laying in his bed with this other woman. Apparently they had fallen asleep. Needless to say, I was hurt." Tears ran down her face, and Robert gave her his handkerchief.

Sniffing, Nancy said, "I'm sorry. I wasn't trying to get you to feel bad for me. It just hurts when I think of what he did after I trusted him. Well, that's enough about my

Life." She dried her eyes and took another drink. "What about you? Weren't you supposed to get

married?"

"Yes," said Robert, "but now I'm trying to get a divorce."

"But Robert," Nancy said, "you just got married. Why are you getting a divorce?" "Well, like you said before, it's a long story. Are you sure you want to hear it?" "Of course," Nancy said.

"Marie and I couldn't get along after we started living together. She left me and went home to her mother."

"You mean she left without a fight?" Nancy asked.

"Yes," said Robert. "I didn't really want her to leave, and I stopped her a few times before, but this time I wasn't going to try to stop her. I sat there and watched her walk out on me. I filed for an uncontested divorce, and she told me she's not going to give it to me. But you know, she never told me what happened to make her change like that."

"Well, I guess we all have problems of some kind," said Nancy. "But for now, cheer up. At least you know you're not alone." They toasted their glasses to the heartaches they held in common. She took one more drink and said, "I have to go now. It was nice seeing you again."

"It was nice seeing you, too," said Robert.

"Hey," he said as Nancy got up from her seat. "Let me walk you to your car." Before she drove off, she pulled out a piece of paper and wrote her phone number on it. She gave it to Robert and said, "If you need to talk to someone, just give me a call."

Robert thought how nice that was of her as he drove home. Going home these nights was hard for Robert because he knew that before going to sleep he would think of Marie. Robert knew that Marie had been trying to get in touch with him, but he didn't return her calls because he was trying to get over her. It was hard, but he was determined to get his life back together. He was going to do it without Marie.

A few weekends later Robert got bored. He was trying to think of going somewhere different instead of going to the bar for drinks. Robert looked in the newspaper in the movie section and saw a movie that he wanted to see. It was one that he had discussed with Nancy. Robert grabbed his wallet and began to search for Nancy's phone number. He found it and gave her a call.

"Hey, this is Robert. You know, your drinking buddy?" he said laughing. "This is a surprise," Nancy said.

"Listen, do you feel up to going to the movies with me later? It's that one we talked about at the bar one night, *Love on a Two-Way Street*."

"Oh, yes," Nancy said, "I'd love to see that movie. My friend and I were talking about it today at work. What time does it start?"

"I hear it's a two-hour movie," said Robert, "so I guess we should be there around seven. Would it be all right if I picked you up at six thirty?"

"Yes. Do you have a pen handy so I can give you my address?" "Hold on a minute," Robert said. He went over to the coffee table and got a pen.

Nancy gave him her address. "Oh good, I know exactly where that is. I shouldn't have any trouble finding your place."

"Well," said Nancy, "I better go now. I have a few things to do. I'll see you at six-Thirty."

Robert arrived at Nancy's apartment at six-fifteen and knocked on the door. "Just a moment," Nancy shouted, as she walked to the door and opened it. "Good evening," said Robert.

"Hi," Nancy said, smiling. "Come on in and make yourself comfortable." She escorted him to the couch. "I'll be ready in just a few minutes," and she went into her bedroom.

"This is a nice apartment you have here," Robert said from the living room. "I'm glad you like it," Nancy said, as she walked back into the living room. She Was dressed in a mini skirt with a flowered blouse. She had put on make-up and wore gold earrings.

Robert cleared his throat. "You look beautiful." Nancy smiled and said, "Thanks. Shall we go now?"

"Oh, yes," Robert said and got up from the couch and walked toward the door. They arrived in just enough time to get popcorn and a good seat. It was a love story that lasted two and a half hours. An hour and a half into the movie, Nancy fell asleep. She laid her head on Robert's shoulder. Robert became immersed in the movie, and at times he would imagine that Nancy was Marie and they were in the movie making love like the actors. In the middle of a lovemaking scene, Nancy woke up. It was late when the movie ended, and Robert and Nancy didn't want to stop for drinks before going home. Robert headed straight for Nancy's apartment. The thought of the lovemaking parts in the movie weighed heavily on his mind. When they arrived at Nancy's apartment, Nancy asked Robert if he would like to come in for a drink before going home.

"Sure," said Robert, "I could use one about now."

Robert sat on the couch while Nancy fixed drinks for them. Giving him his drink, she sat beside him. They talked about the movie as they drank. After a few drinks, Robert began to feel more comfortable.

In an effort to control himself, he held Nancy's hand and said, "Thanks for going to the movie with me and having me over. I guess I'll be leaving now."

"Thank you," said Nancy. "The movie was great, but do you really have to leave?"

"Well, not really. I don't have anything else to do, but I didn't want to overstay my welcome either."

"Then stay a little while longer," said Nancy. "And don't worry. I won't let you overstay your welcome."

Robert sat back on the couch beside Nancy and continued to drink. "You know," he said, "you're a good person, and I like the way I feel when I'm around you."

"How do you feel?" asked Nancy.

"I feel good," Robert admitted.

"I feel good when I'm around you, too," Nancy said, blushing. "I've been lonely these past few weeks," said Robert. "It feels good to have someone to talk to, someone who'll spend time with me, and listen to what I'm saying." He looked into Nancy's eyes.

"I've told you before, you don't have to beat around the bush with me," she said, She moved her face closer to his. "I know you like me, and I like you. In so many words, we've told each other that." She leaned forward and kissed him on the lips. Her hands moved across his chest.

"Relax," Nancy, said when Robert remained tense. "It doesn't have to mean anymore than we make of it, so enjoy yourself." They kissed more. They both seemed hungry for love. Robert laid her back on the couch. He lay down beside her. He kissed her, and he looked into her eyes as he unbuttoned her blouse and exposed her beautiful, smooth skin. She moaned as he kissed one shoulder and stroked the other one with his hand. She began to sigh as Robert massaged her from her shoulder to her ear with his tongue. With one hand, he began to massage her breast as he kissed her lips. His erection was hard as he pressed his body against hers. He pulled down her bra and began to kiss her breasts. He sucked her nipples like he couldn't get enough. With his hand, he began to massage her stomach and her thighs. He pushed up her skirt and felt the softness of her muff.

Nancy began to moan as she arched her body toward his hand. As his fingers slipped down, he felt heat and softness through her panties. It was then that he pulled her panties aside, and his middle finger slipped into her vagina.

Nancy cried, "Give it to me! Give it to me now!"

Robert could hold back no longer. He pulled off her panties, and Nancy opened her legs to invite him into her, moaning and arching her body. Robert rolled on top of her, kissing and sucking her tongue. He moved between her legs.

"Oh, please put it in," Nancy said. "Put it in me now. I want you, Robert." Robert was content to let his erection find its own way inside her, as they pressed harder against each other.

Robert was breathing hard as he whispered, "It feels so good, and I want it to Last."

"Oh, Robert. Do I make you feel good?" Nancy murmured, as she moved her body to keep pace with Robert's movements. Suddenly Robert slipped into her. "Oh, yes," Nancy moaned. "That's what I want."

Robert moved slowly, pulling in and out.

"I hope it feels as good to you as it does to me," Nancy said, as she arched her body forward to accept Robert's stroke.

"Yes, it does. It feels so good," Robert murmured, as he stroked harder and sank deeper into her.

Robert and Nancy stopped moving. Nancy arched her body to receive Robert's whole member. They pressed hard against each other and yelled with pleasure as their juices flowed. Robert felt relief from his arousal, and without realizing it, he whispered, "Oh, Marie."

Chapter 7

"What did you call me?" Nancy asked. She pushed him away, looking into his
Eyes.

"I didn't call you anything," Robert said.

Nancy got up. As she put on her clothes, she said, "What were you doing? Were you having sex with Marie or me?"

"I'm sorry," said Robert. "I haven't had sex with anyone since Marie and I broke up. I don't know what happened." Robert held his head down in shame.

"Look. Don't worry about it," Nancy said. "I told you before we started that it didn't have to mean anything. We were just two people who were lonely and attracted to each other. We had sex. That's it. It doesn't mean anything. I enjoyed it, and I hope you did also."

"Well, I guess I'll go home now," Robert said. "I've caused enough disappointment for one night."

"Don't leave now. You may as well spend the rest of the morning here. That is, if you don't have any place to be that's more important. You can sleep on the couch, and I'll sleep in my bedroom. And besides, I really don't want to be alone. I'll get you some bedding."

Nancy got up and went into the bathroom. Robert sat on the couch feeling sorry for himself. He realized that he was still in love with Marie. He felt uneasy because he had never had sex with a woman he wasn't in love with, and he had no idea that it could feel so good.

When Nancy came out of the bathroom with the bedding, she reassured him that he had no reason to feel guilty. They were just friends helping each other during bad times, and she wasn't expecting any form of commitment as a result of having had sex with him.

"Now get some sleep. Goodnight. I'm going to bed." Nancy went into her bedroom and closed the door behind her. Robert prepared the couch with the bedding to sleep.

Nancy was lying in bed thinking of how good Robert had made her feel. No one had ever made her feel that good, not even Richard, who she had sex with for two years. Nancy wasn't the type to sleep around, and she had only been involved in two major relationships. She thought having sex with Robert made her feel different. She felt that Robert was really trying to please her as well as him. She felt like a real woman, responding to a real man that desired her because she was who she was.

Nancy knew that she couldn't let Robert know she had deep feelings for him. After all, he was married, whether he was living with his wife or not. Nancy didn't want to come between Robert and his wife, for fear of losing his friendship and trust. On that thought, Nancy finally fell asleep.

Robert woke up the next morning in time to go home and get some weekend work done. He didn't want to wake Nancy, so he left her apartment quietly, leaving behind a note. He wrote *I'll call you later. Friends always, Robert.*

Since Marie had not seen or talked to Robert for about two weeks, her days had been bad, and her nights had been sleepless. She still loved Robert, and she wasn't going to give him up no matter what. *If Robert won't come to see me,* Marie thought, *I'll go to him.*

Marie got dressed early one morning and drove to Robert's house. When she got there, she saw him mowing the lawn. She pulled up to the sidewalk, put the car in park, and sat there watching him. She hoped that he would notice her and come over to the car and talk. But Robert went on mowing around the other side of the house, out of Marie's sight. Marie drove away without talking to Robert, with the intention of returning later that day.

As she drove down the street, she saw one of Robert's friends that she hadn't seen for a long time. Marie pulled over to the sidewalk and said, "Hello, Mitchell."

"Hello, Marie," said Mitchell. "How are you? How's Robert?" Marie told Mitchell that she had just seen Robert, and he was doing fine. Mitchell was in a hurry, running an errand. He asked Marie to tell Robert that he was going to be at Mike's bar tonight night. He wanted to see Robert and have a few drinks with him before he returned to Denver.

"Okay," said Marie, "I'll tell him."

Marie said good-bye and drove away. When she got home, she waited a while, and then dialed Robert's number, intending to tell him what Mitchell had said. Robert didn't answer, and she didn't leave a message.

Since Marie wasn't able to get in touch with Robert by phone, she decided she would go down to the bar early that evening. Maybe she would see him there and be able to talk with him. The last time Marie had been to Mike's Bar was the time she thought she saw Robert kissing another woman, an event still clear in her mind.

Robert finished mowing the lawn at four thirty. He decided he would give Nancy a call like he had said on his note.

"I got the note you left for me this morning. Did you sleep well on the couch last night?" Nancy asked.

"I sure did," said Robert.

Robert wanted to talk about them having had sex last night, but before he could bring it up, Nancy said, "Don't worry about what happened last night. It'll take care of itself. I slept well, better than I've slept in quite a while. So let's just leave it at that, okay?"

"Okay," Robert said. "Hey, listen. I'm going to Mike's bar this evening. Would you like to come? The drinks are on me.

"You go ahead," said Nancy. "I'll be there, but I'll be a little late, so save a seat for me."

"Okay, I'll see you there."

Marie fixed her face and put on a dress that Robert liked, and then she headed to the bar. Mitchell was already there. Mitchell saw her when she entered and invited her to sit at his table with some of his friends. Mitchell introduced her as she sat down. When the waitress came to take their orders, Marie ordered a soda.

An hour later, Nancy came and sat at the bar. She called the bartender over and asked him if Robert had been in today. The bartender told her no.

Robert had overslept and was late leaving for the bar. When he arrived, he walked in and saw Nancy sitting in their usual spot. He didn't pay much attention to any of the people who were sitting at the tables. Robert walked over and greeted her with a kiss on her cheek and sat next to her. He didn't see Marie when he walked into the bar, and Marie didn't see him. The bartender knew Robert and Nancy because they were his favorite customers. They always sat together in the bar, and they always tipped him when they left.

He also knew that Marie was Robert's wife and that she was in the bar, too. He wanted to warn Nancy of that fact, but he decided against it. He thought it was none of

His business. Robert ordered drinks for the both of them and noticed there were lots of people at the bar. The bartender kept his mouth shut and served the drinks hoping that nothing would happen.

After a few drinks, Nancy and Robert were high as a kite. Marie was walking toward the ladies' room when Robert saw her, but she didn't seem to see him. He was somewhat surprised that she was in the bar because when they were together, she promised him that she wouldn't take another drink, at least until their child was born.

He was angry that Marie was drinking, possibly harming herself and his child. *I'm not going to sit here and let that happen,* he thought, as he ordered another drink. Robert made up his mind that when Marie came out of the ladies' room, he was going to confront her. When Marie stepped through the door, Robert saw her and in his mind she was the most beautiful sight he had ever seen. He lost all the anger that he was feeling and forgot about confronting her. He held his head down so she wouldn't notice him as she walked back to her table and sat down.

"Is there something wrong?" asked Nancy.

"I don't know anymore," Robert said sadly. "Sometimes I feel as if I'm losing my mind or something."

"Well," said Nancy, "if you'd like to talk about it, I'm here for you. After all, what are friends for?"

"I know," said Robert, "but I've bothered you enough with my problems." "Nonsense," Nancy said, taking a drink. "If something's bothering you, you need to talk about it. You'll feel better."

Robert told Nancy that Marie was in the bar. "She's sitting at the table across the bar with her back turned to us."

Nancy looked in the direction where Marie was sitting, but she could only see the back of Marie's head.

"Well," said Nancy," as far as I can see, she does have beautiful hair. Why don't you introduce her to me?"

"Oh no," said Robert. "She might take things the wrong way, and I may have to explain us to her."

"What do you mean explain us to her?" Nancy said. "There is no explaining. Can't you have friends? If you won't introduce me, I'll just go over and introduce myself."

"Please don't do that," Robert said. "I'll introduce you to her another time." "Okay," said Nancy, "but I think you should at least go over and say hi to her." "In a little while," Robert said.

"Oh, I get it," said Nancy, "you want to see who she's with, don't you?" "No, that's not it. Marie can be with who ever she wants. We're separated, and I
Don't have any say about anyone she wants to be with. My concern is for our child. She shouldn't be out drinking while she's pregnant."

"Oh, you didn't tell me a child was involved. How far along is she?" Nancy asked.

"I don't know for sure," Robert said stupidly.

"Then why don't you go over and tell her how you feel?" Nancy suggested. "Here, take another drink. Then go over there and tell her what you think about her drinking."

Robert swallowed the drink and began walking toward Marie's table. As he came closer, he could see that Marie was sitting with his old friend, Mitchell, who he hadn't seen in a long time.

Robert approached the table and said, "Hello everyone." Mitchell got up, saying, "Robert, is that you, old buddy?" He came over to Robert, hugged him, and shook his hand.

"Man, it's been a long time," Robert said. "Where are you living these days? Are you here to stay?"

"Well," Mitchell started, "I'm living in Denver now, and I came down two days ago to visit my mother. I've been trying to find you ever since I got here. Finally, I saw Marie and asked her to give you the message that I was going to be here tonight, and here you are. Damn, it's good to see you again, buddy. Pull up a chair and sit down. Have a drink or two."

Robert pulled up a chair and sat next to Marie. He controlled his anger because he didn't want to argue with Marie in front of his old friend. Robert avoided talking to Marie while his friend was at the table, and she avoided talking to him as well. Then he thought of Nancy. He had left her sitting at the bar.

"I'll be right back," Robert said. Nancy wasn't in her seat. He called the bartender over and asked if he knew what happened to Nancy.

"Oh," the bartender replied, "she left."

"Okay, thanks," Robert said. He hoped Nancy wouldn't hold it against him. *Oh well,* he thought, *I'll call her later and explain what happened.*

Robert returned to the table and sat down. At about midnight Mitchell said, "It's been nice seeing you guys again, but it's time for me to go home. My wife's going to kill me. Robert, before I leave, I want to get your phone number so I can keep in touch."

"Okay, I'll give it to you right now." Robert pulled out a pen, wrote his number on a napkin, and gave it to Mitchell. Robert and Marie were left alone at the table. Robert turned toward Marie and said, "Well, how's it been going with you."

"Okay," said Marie, "no thanks to you. I've been trying to get in touch with you for the past two weeks, but you never answer the phone."

"Listen, I'm not going to fight with you tonight. We're separated and I'm tired. I'm going home and going to bed." Robert got up from the table.

Marie grabbed his hand as he got up and said, "Please don't leave yet. I'm sorry if I made you mad, but I need to talk to you."

Robert sat back down. "Okay, what do you want to talk about?" "Us, you, me, our child," she said.

"You're out here drinking, knowing you could be causing our child damage, and yet you have the nerve to want to talk to me about it?"

"You've got it all wrong. I'm not drinking. I came here tonight expecting to find you so I could give you the message from Mitchell. I've been trying to get in touch with you by phone, but there was no answer, so I figured if I came down to the bar early I'd at least get a chance to talk to you. As far as drinking is concerned, I haven't had a drink since I promised you I'd stop. Here." She held her cup to Robert's nose.

"It's soda. I was only drinking soda," Marie said. She began to cry. Robert handed Marie his handkerchief.

"Don't embarrass me," Robert said. "You know I can't stand to see you cry."

"I'm sorry," Marie muttered through the handkerchief, "but I love you, and I'll always love you no matter what. I even came by your house when you were mowing the lawn, but I didn't get out because I thought you were too busy to talk. I know we have some differences, but we can work them out. I can't give you up, not now."

"Do we have to talk about this now? I'm tired, and you should get some rest also," Robert said.

"Okay, but first you must promise me that you'll call me tomorrow." "Alright, I'll call you tomorrow." Robert began to get up from the table. Marie got up after him and said, "Well, aren't you going to walk me to my car?" "Sure, ok."

Robert said goodnight to Marie at her car.

Robert woke up about noon the next day. He was thinking about Nancy and how he had left her sitting at the bar the night before. Even though he had talked to Marie, he didn't say what he intended to say. He thought of how Nancy had coaxed him into talking to Marie when he didn't really have the nerve. Robert called Nancy.

"Hello," Nancy said.

"What happened to you last night?" Robert began.

"Well, I knew you'd be busy talking with your wife, so I decided not to wait for you to return, and I drove home."

"Well, I left shortly afterward," said Robert. "You mean you didn't go home with your wife?"

"Oh no, I drove to my house last night. I was so tired that I went to bed without taking my clothes off. I didn't get the chance to call you. That's the reason for calling you today. I was hoping that you didn't get offended by me asking you out and leaving you sitting at the bar the way I did."

"Think nothing of it. After all, you did tell me you were leaving before you left, and besides, I encouraged you to go," she said, laughing. "You were so drunk and disgusted about your wife that I knew you needed to talk with her."

"Hey," Robert said. "Are you going down to the bar tonight?" "No, I'm not feeling well, so I think I'll pass it up tonight." "What's wrong? Robert asked sadly.

"Nothing really," said Nancy. "I just want to give it a rest for tonight." "Well, okay. Would it be all right if I called you later?" "Sure, but don't call very late because I'll be asleep," Nancy said.

Later that evening, Robert got dressed to go to the bar. He forgot to call Marie. He thought being at the bar wasn't going to be much fun without Nancy being there to talk to and drink with, so he decided to rent a movie, buy a pizza, and go over to her apartment to try to cheer her up.

Marie was very upset that Robert didn't call her and decided to take matters into her own hands by visiting him.

As she approached Robert's house, she saw him walk out the front door and get into his car. As he drove away, Marie followed him, but not closely enough for him to notice. He drove to the video store and got a movie, and then he stopped at the pizza parlor. He then turned a corner. When he arrived at Nancy's, he left the pizza and the movie in the car while he went into the apartment building. Marie parked farther down the street, watching.

Marie thought Robert must have been seeing someone in that building, so she sat watching Robert's car for a while.

Robert walked down the hallway to Nancy's apartment and knocked on the door. "Who is it?" Nancy asked.

"Open the door and see," Robert said.

Nancy knew Robert's voice, so she opened the door and let him in. "What are you doing here?" asked Nancy. "I thought you'd be at the bar by now having a drink or something."

"Well, being at the bar wasn't going to be fun if you weren't there. And since you weren't

feeling well, I thought I might just come over and try to cheer you up a little. I brought pizza and a movie, but I left them in the car until I found out if you were home. I'll go down and get them. That is, if you don't have anything else planned."

Nancy smiled and shook her head, as she said, "No, I don't have anything else planned." She gave Robert a key to the door.

"Let yourself in when you get back," Nancy said. Nancy went into the other room to freshen up. Marie watched as he took out the pizza and the movie and returned to the building. She stayed parked near the sidewalk, watching Robert's car for another hour before going home.

Robert and Nancy sat on the couch in Nancy's apartment and ate pizza while they watched the movie. When the movie was over and all the pizza was gone, Robert stood up and stretched. He said, "I think it's time for me to leave. I need to go home and get some rest before work in the morning."

Nancy stood up, put her arms around Robert's neck, and said, "Thanks for the movie and the pizza, and thanks for thinking of me." She looked into Robert's eyes and kissed him, and then she said goodnight.

"I'll call you tomorrow after work," Robert said.

Nancy leaned against the door after Robert left for a few minutes with a smile on her face.

Robert drove home listening to his car radio, feeling happy. When he got home, he undressed. While removing the change from his pockets, he noticed that he still had Nancy's door key with him. His thought was to get dressed again and take the key back to her, but instead he decided to call.

"Hello," Nancy said softly.

"This is Robert. I didn't mean to disturb you, but I forgot to give you your key back before I left. If you need it tonight, I can bring it to you."

"Oh, it's not necessary. I have another key. You need to get some rest for work. You can give me the key tomorrow."

"Are you sure?" Robert asked. "Yes," said Nancy.

"Okay then, I'll talk to you later. Goodnight." "Goodnight," Nancy said.

The next evening when Robert got off work, he called Nancy and asked if she could meet him at Mike's Bar in order for him to return her key. Nancy agreed, so Robert showered and dressed. As he stepped out of the shower the phone rang.

"This is Marie. I'm calling to talk with you about us," she began. "I don't have time to talk right now," Robert said.

Marie hung up the phone. All she could think of was Robert seeing another woman. She borrowed her friend's car and drove to the street where Robert lived. His car was parked in his yard, so she assumed he was still at home. Marie parked at a distance, where Robert couldn't see her, and she waited for him to come out. Soon, Robert came out and got into his car. He drove to

Mike's Bar. Marie followed him and watched him get out of his car and go into the bar. She parked and waited. Since it was a Monday, a slow night at the bar, only two cars were in the parking lot. One of them belonged to Robert and the other one belonged to the bartender. Judging by the cars, she decided to wait until the next car showed up before going inside.

As she sat there waiting, another car drove into the lot. Marie watched the woman who got out and walked into the bar. *That's the same woman I saw Robert kissing,* Marie thought. Marie became so angry that she began to cry. She kicked her door open, grabbed a brick, walked up to Robert's car, and threw the brick through the windshield. That calmed her down a little. *I'm going in there to tell that woman to leave my husband alone.*

Chapter 8

When Nancy went into the bar, she sat next to Robert. Here's your key," Robert
Said.

As he reached into his pocket to get it, Nancy said, "Why don't you just hold onto it for a while? You never know when you might want to come over for pizza."

She smiled, so Robert left the key in his pocket and continued to drink. Just as Nancy placed her hand on Robert's leg, Marie walked through the door. She hesitated for a moment, looking directly at Robert and Nancy. The bartender cleared his throat loudly to get Robert's attention as Marie walked toward him looking angry. He could see she had tears in her eyes. Robert froze, and so did Nancy.

Marie asked Robert, "Is this the woman that you were sleeping with before we got married? Is this the one that you're deserting your wife and child for? Why didn't you marry her instead?" she cried.

Robert got up from the bar and nervously asked Marie if they could go outside and talk.

"Talk? I've been trying to get in touch with you for three weeks so we could talk. You had the nerve to tell me when I called you today that you'd talk to me some other time. Now you want to talk to me, is that it? Well I don't think so!"

Marie looked over at Nancy and said, "Listen, you, I saw you with my husband before we got married, and now you're with him again. You better watch your back or one day you might find that something's sticking in it." Marie's face grew red.

"I want you to know there's a law against making threats like that," Nancy said, as she got up from her seat. "And as far as me watching my back, there's enough people

Doing that for me." Nancy walked out of the bar, swinging her hips seductively. When she got to the door, she looked back and said, "I'll see you later, Robert."

Marie turned to Robert and said, "I suppose you want to go outside and kiss her good-bye, don't you? Well, go ahead. You did it before we were married, so do it again now that we're separated. I don't give a damn what you do anymore. Bartender, give me a drink please."

Robert held his hand up to stop the bartender. Robert put his arms around Marie and said, "Listen, I know you're angry about what you think you saw, but it just didn't happen that way. I never went to bed with Nancy before you and I were married, and I never kissed her in the parking

lot. I walked her to her car, but I never kissed her. We're just good friends, that's all."

Robert gave Marie his handkerchief to dry her eyes. Then he said, "You told me Sunday night that you stopped drinking, and before then you said you wouldn't take another drink until our child was born. Why are you asking for one now? If I'm the reason you want to take a drink, then I'll just leave because I'm not worth the hurt and humiliation that you're trying to put yourself through. You've worked hard and been through so much trying to defeat your alcoholism. Don't you see, Marie, it would be beneath you to go down now. Let's go to a table and sit down so we can talk."

He held one arm around her shoulders as he led her to a table. Robert said, "Bartender, two Cokes, please." He turned to Marie and said, "I beg you, Marie, don't start drinking."

"Why should you care?" Marie asked, sniffling. "You don't have to be around me when I'm drinking."

"I know," said Robert, "but I love you, and I care about our child." Marie barely stopped herself from crying. She said, "If you love me and care
About us so much, then why are you running around with another woman? Why aren't you with me and your baby?"

"Nancy's not that other woman," said Robert. "She's just a friend, someone to talk to rather than sitting around being lonely."

"If she's just a friend," said Marie, "do you spend the night with her?" Robert dropped his head in shame and murmured, "I don't know what you're
Talking about."

"I know about you and your so-called friend. And I know you spent Saturday night with her, so just cut the bull. What were you thinking with, that thing in your pants? I had made up my mind to fight for you because I love you and you're my husband. I wanted our marriage to work, but seeing you sitting here with your friend, the friend that you spend the night with from time to time, I feel I've loved nothing but a dream, a dream that we could live together and love each other forever. Now all of that has changed. You can sleep with your friend as many nights as you like, and you can ask your lawyer to mail me the divorce papers because I'm ready to sign them." Marie got up from the table and walked out of the bar.

Robert didn't leave right away. He sat there feeling sorry for himself and tried to figure out where he went wrong. Finally, Robert thought to himself, "I might as well go home."

When he got to his car, he noticed that there was broken glass all over the trunk, and he saw that his back window was broken. He put two and two together and knew

Marie must have done it. Robert walked to the driver's side of his car and unlocked the door. He brushed the broken glass from the front seat, got in, and drove home. When Robert got home, he parked in his backyard and went to his storage shed to find some plastic to cover the car window. After he covered it, he went inside to think. Robert felt bad that his conversation with Marie had ended with harsh feelings. He wanted the divorce, but he didn't want to be shut out of his child's life, even if it meant getting back together with Marie.

Robert called Marie, but she only said, "I have nothing more to say to you" before hanging up. Now he was beginning to understand how it felt when someone you loved refused to talk to you. Life wasn't worth living anymore. He lay in his bed thinking of something that Marie said to him once: "You're my husband, and I'm not going to let you go. I love you."

He thought, *well, she's not going to get away that easily. I'm not going to let her go, either.* After a lengthy time of lying in the bed, smoking cigarette after cigarette, he finally fell asleep. The next morning, Robert woke up late for work. Once again he took the day off. Most of that day, he walked the floor thinking of Marie and not eating. Marie was probably at work, and Robert didn't want to call her because she wouldn't have enough time for him to say what he needed to. He decided to wait until she got off work.

Pacing the floor, he thought of blaming Nancy for his problems with Marie, but he thought, *Nancy never asked me to go anywhere or do anything. And that night, when I went to bed with her, I went because I waned to, not because she wanted me to.* When he thought Marie would be home from work, Robert called her.

Marie's friend answered the phone. "Marie isn't here at the moment. Would you like to leave a message?"

"No, I'll call her back later." Robert thought, *where could she be? I need to talk with her.*

Robert paced the floor and watched TV for two hours. Then he called Marie again. This time there was no answer. As he waited for another chance to get in touch with Marie, he began to feel sick and weak. He lay down for a while and went to sleep. He didn't wake up until the next morning, again too late to get to work on time. He called in sick. He thought maybe it was because he wasn't eating. He went to the kitchen and fixed breakfast and forced the food down. Within the hour, everything that Robert ate came back up. He was too weak to walk, but he made his way to the bed and lay down. *I should call an ambulance and have them take me to the emergency room.*

Robert called 911 and gave them the necessary information, and they said they were on their way. Robert managed to get dressed as he waited for them to arrive. When Mobile Medic got to Robert's house, he made an attempt to let them in, but he passed out as he opened the front door. He was dripping with sweat and breathing abnormally.

They put him on a stretcher and got him to the hospital. After the doctor examined him, he needed a signature before he could give Robert any further treatment. They needed his spouse to come to the hospital. Marie got a call from medical records at the hospital. They told her that Robert had been admitted and that he was unconscious. Although Marie was frightened she told the clerk that she would be right down. Marie grabbed her keys, rushed out to the car, and drove to the hospital. When she got to the emergency room, they let her sign treatment papers for Robert and asked that she wait for

A few minutes before she would be allowed to go into intensive care where Robert was recovering.

When Marie was finally let into the room, she saw Robert lying in the bed with his eyes closed. The nurse told Marie that Robert would be sleeping for a while because of the medication. Marie decided to sit with him anyway. While she watched Robert sleeping, she thought of the lovely moments they had once shared. Marie gripped Robert's hand, and then she looked toward heaven and said, "Oh, God, please let Robert be okay. I love him so much." Marie became tired and leaned back in her chair and fell asleep, holding Robert's hand. When Robert woke up a few hours later, he turned his head and saw Marie sitting next to him. Marie woke up. She looked at Robert and saw that he was smiling as he squeezed her hand.

"Good morning," she said with a smile. "How are you feeling?" "I feel much better now that I know you're here," Robert said weakly. The doctor walked into the room with a nurse. They said good morning to Marie
And Robert. The doctor asked, "How are you feeling this morning, Robert?"

"Fine," he said, and he looked at Marie. The doctor asked him if he remembered what happened. Robert told him everything up to the point at which he passed out. After that, he didn't remember anything until he woke up this morning.

"Judging from the tests that we did," said the doctor, "you had a flu virus. What did you eat before coming to the hospital?"

Robert said, "The day before I came to the hospital, I didn't eat anything because I didn't have an appetite. And later I felt too sick to eat anything. On the day that I came to the hospital, I ate breakfast, and it came back up."

"That explains why you passed out," the doctor said. "You were suffering from a lack of nutrients, and now that we see the medication we gave you is working well, I see no reason to hold you here. I'm going to write up a discharge order for you, and I'm going to give you a prescription for some antibiotics, which you need to take twice a day until they're gone. Tomorrow I want you to call my office and make an appointment to come in for a visit in two weeks so I can check you over and see how you're doing."

"Okay," said Robert. "What time do you think the discharge will be ready?" "I'm going to order it now, so it should be ready about noon. I'm happy to have
Been able to help, and if there's anything else I can do for you, just let me know. I'll see you in two weeks. It was nice meeting you, Marie. Take care of Robert."

"Good-bye," Marie said.

"Thank you, Doctor," Robert said.

Robert sat up in bed and asked Marie how she knew he was in the hospital. "The hospital contacted me in order to get a signature for treatment," she said. "I see," said Robert. "Is that the only reason you came to see me?"

Marie placed her hand on top of his and said, "If I ever made you think that I didn't care about you, I'm sorry because I didn't mean to. I've always cared about you, and I still do. It hurt me when I saw you hugging that other woman before we were married."

"You saw me?" Robert asked in disbelief.

"Someone called my house that day and told me that you and that woman were planning to meet at Mike's bar that night. You didn't tell me that you were going out, so I decided to see for myself. I borrowed my friend's car and parked it across the street from the bar. I waited for you to come out, and that's when I saw you and that woman together. I didn't mean to spy on you and I trusted you, but when I got that message over the phone, I had to see it for myself before I could believe it. There I was watching the man I was going to marry cheat on me. I hardly knew what to do after that. I wanted to tell you about what I saw, but I didn't want you to think I was being possessive.

"I decided to go along with the wedding and hoped after we were married things would get better, but they didn't. Every day I would hurt, thinking of how you mistreated me, and even asked you for a divorce when I didn't really want one."

Robert said, "I love you, Marie. You're the light of my life, and you must believe me when I tell you I would never intentionally do anything to hurt you. To me, you're my dream come true. And as far as that night's concerned, that didn't mean anything. I was only trying to be helpful. I had just met Nancy at the bar a few days before. You and I weren't on good terms, and I was lonely and needed someone to talk to. I had a few drinks, and then Nancy walked into the bar. When she sat down, I offered to buy her a drink, and she accepted. She and I and the bartender got into a conversation. I couldn't hear well, so I moved over to the seat next to her so that the three of us could talk. The discussion lasted for the rest of the night. There's no telling how much we drank.

"When it was time for the bar to close, Nancy got up from the stool and staggered. I was pretty drunk myself, but I got up and held her by her shoulders until she could get her balance. The bartender asked if I could walk her to her car because he didn't want to see her fall and hurt herself. Every night after that, Nancy and I wound up sitting at Mike's drinking and talking. And when we got ready to leave, I would walk her to her car. We became so regular that the bartender would tell me goodnight and to make sure Nancy got to her car, even when we weren't drunk."

Marie didn't say anything, so Robert continued. "The way I see it, the person who called you that night was Nancy's boyfriend or one of his friends. I say that because I remember Nancy telling me once that she had a boyfriend named Richard. Then after we got married and separated, I saw Nancy again at the bar, and she told me that she and Richard had broken up. When I asked her what happened, she said he accused her of seeing another man and that the man she was seeing was me. Apparently, someone other than you had seen Nancy and me leaving the bar together. I understand the part where you said you saw me walking Nancy to her car, but I never kissed her."

Marie felt better now that she and Robert were at least talking. "So let's just forget about all that for now. Do you have a way home?" Marie asked.

"No, I don't," said Robert. "I guess I'll have to catch a taxi." "Oh, that won't be necessary. I'll give you a ride."

"I'd appreciate that," he said with a smile. "I'm going to get dressed." He stood up and said, "I could use some coffee."

"I'll go to the nurses' station to see if they have some," Marie said. When she walked back into the room, she said, "The nurse said it was okay for you to have coffee this morning, so I brought you a cup."

"Thanks," Robert said, taking the cup.

They sat there and talked until the time came for Robert to be discharged. The nurse in charge came and asked Robert to sit in a wheelchair.

"Thanks, but I don't need that. I can walk on my own," he said.

"I don't think so," said the nurse. "Hospital policy says that every patient discharged from the hospital must be escorted by medical personnel and, in your case, in a wheelchair, so don't argue with me." Robert knew that arguing would be pointless and got into the wheelchair. The nurse placed the discharge papers in his lap, and the three of them headed for the front exit.

On their way to Robert's house, Robert appeared much better. For a while there was silence as they drove. Then Robert said, "You know, some people don't realize how good it feels to be in good health until they've been really sick. On the other hand, they don't miss their water until their

well has run dry. I guess I'm using these phrases to lead to what I really want to say, which is I missed you very much."

Marie glanced over at Robert and smiled. Robert continued, "You're my water, and when you're not with me, I miss you. My well is dry, and you know a person can't last too long without water."

Marie took a deep breath and said, "Oh, stop it, Robert. You have no well that's going to run dry, and as far as water is concerned, there's plenty to last us. By the way, don't you need to stop to get your prescription filled?"

"That's right. There's a drugstore about three blocks ahead, and if you don't mind, you can stop there."

"You know I don't mind."

They pulled into the parking lot. "Do you need me to go in and get your prescription for you?" Marie asked.

"No, I'll get it. Besides, it will only take a few minutes because the doctor already called it in. You can come along with me to keep me from falling down," he said jokingly.

Marie laughed and said, "You're full of it this morning."

They got Robert's medicine and headed to his house. When they got there, Robert asked Marie to help him inside. Once inside, Marie closed the door, and as she turned around, Robert put his arms around her and kissed her. Marie pushed away and asked, "What are you doing?"

Robert said, "Okay, I was faking being unable to get into my house because I wanted you to come in instead of going home."

He held his head down, but Marie lifted it up. She kissed Robert and said, "I knew that. I was waiting for you to ask me in before you started your little game." They both walked into the living room and sat on the couch. Marie began to look around the room. She asked, "May I take a look around?"

"Go right ahead," Robert said. Marie got up and started looking around. When Marie walked into the bedroom, she saw that Robert had clothes scattered all over the floor.

"Robert!" she shouted. "Could you come in here a minute please?" Robert went to her. Marie said, as if she was fussing at him, "Why do you have all of these clothes scattered in your room like this? You know better."

"Well, I left in such a hurry for the hospital that I didn't have time to clean up," Robert said, and he began to pick up his pants.

"Oh, sure, give me those pants and go into the living room and sit down and rest. I'll clean this place up a little."

"Yes, Mom," said Robert, and quickly kissed her again. It tasted good. They kissed again, and this time they held each other in their arms, and their tongues met. Marie broke the kiss and said, "I missed you so much."

"I missed you, too," said Robert. They kissed madly, and they pulled at each other's clothes. Robert laid her on the bed craving her love. Marie opened her legs, and he put himself inside her. One movement of her hips and they both climaxed. They lay in the bed and held each other.

Marie got up and went to the bathroom to wash up. When Robert got up, he picked up his pants, and a key fell out of his pocket. Robert looked at the key and then looked to see if Marie had noticed it. He took the key and thought; *I'll put it up on the shed key ring.* He walked out of the room quickly, hoping that Marie didn't see the key because it would be hard for him to explain how Nancy's key got into his pocket.

When Marie was finished with the cleaning, she fixed food for Robert to eat later. Then she went into the living room and sat on the couch next to him. Robert was very quiet. He listened to the words that came out of her mouth, hoping that it wouldn't be anything about a key. "Robert, I don't want you to be offended by this, but did you tell Nancy about us?" Marie asked.

"Of course," Robert said. "She knows that I love you very much. When Nancy and I were talking, we were talking about you."

"Really? What are some of the things that you were saying?" Marie asked. "Well, just things like how I wish we could solve our problems and get back together."

"And what did she say to that?" Marie probed.

"She said that if I really loved you, I should keep trying to get back together with you and never give up hope."

"Are you sure she said all that?" "Yes, I'm sure," said Robert.

Marie looked at the clock and said, "I told Mother I'd stop by the store and pick up a few things for her on my way back home."

Robert put his arms around her and said, "Don't leave now, please." "I'm sorry, but I must get to the store before they close." "Okay then. I'll walk you to the door."

They got up from the couch and walked toward the front door. As Marie was leaving, she said, "Maybe we can get together later when I can stay longer."

Robert smiled and said, "Okay, I'd like that."

When Marie left, Robert thought about Nancy's key. He thought he'd call her up to see if he could return it that evening. He rushed to the telephone and dialed Nancy's number.

"Hello, Nancy. This is Robert."

Nancy hesitated and said, "What's up? I haven't heard from you since the incident at Mike's Bar. I assume everything worked out."

"I'm doing fine after a short stay in the hospital." "What happened? Did Marie mess you up that badly?"

"No, it wasn't Marie. The doctor said I had the flu and that I was dehydrated. They kept me in the hospital for a day."

"Why didn't you call me?" Nancy said. "I would have come to visit you."

"Well, I wasn't exactly in my right mind," said Robert. "I'm as solid as a rock now," he said. He thought how nice it was that Marie was there for him. "Before I forget, I want to give you your key back, and I called to find out if you were at home so I could bring it over."

"Did Marie tell you that you couldn't keep it?"

"No," said Robert, "I wanted to return it because I don't think I'll have any use for it."

"Are you dumping me now that you've got Marie back?" she asked accusingly. "It's not that. Marie and I aren't back together yet. But now I'm beginning to think that there is a chance for us, and I don't want anything to spoil that chance. Just so I don't have to explain this key to her, I'm returning it to you."

"I understand," Nancy said. Her voice dripped with disappointment. "Why don't you bring the key over tomorrow evening at seven?"

"Okay, I'll call you before I come."

Chapter 9

The next day Robert called his job and got the rest of the week off. He planned to spend it with Marie. That day, Robert stayed busy doing things around the house, waiting for evening to come so he would be able to see his wife. At five o'clock, he decided to give Nancy her key early. Robert called Nancy and told her that he was on his way over.

"Okay, but could you bring me a soda when you come?" Nancy asked. "Sure, no problem," Robert said. He hurried out the door and into his car and drove away.

Nancy had stalled him by asking him to bring her a soda because, counting the time that it took for him to stop at the store, it would give her enough time to be ready when he arrived. Nancy dimmed the lights and placed candles on the table. She chilled the wine and placed some soft music into the CD player. *Tonight,* she thought, *I'm going to have him whether he wants me or not. I'm not going to let Marie get in my way.*

Robert knocked on the door. "Use your key and come in," Nancy said. Robert unlocked the door and walked into the apartment. He didn't see anyone, so he called out for Nancy.

"I'm in the dining room," she said in her sweetest voice.

When Robert walked into the dining room, he saw that the candles were lit and the lights were dimmed. Nancy had on a see-through dress and was standing in front of a floodlight that silhouetted the shape of her body. The music was playing softly, and Nancy was moving from side to

side, rubbing her waist and thighs. Robert stood in a daze watching her. Nancy grabbed a glass of wine from the table and walked toward Robert. She held the glass up to his lips, and before he could say anything, she said, "Sip." Robert took a sip, and Nancy kissed him and pressed her body up against him, moving with the beat of the music. As she lowered the glass, she took a sip and kissed Robert again. This time, she let the wine run from her mouth into Robert's mouth. Robert almost forgot why he had come to Nancy's apartment, and the more Nancy kissed him, the more he thought about how good it was making him feel. He wanted to resist Nancy, but instead he thought, *what the heck? One more time won't hurt.*

Robert forgot about the key, he forgot about Marie, and he even forgot about himself. The only thing he could think about was Nancy and what she was doing to him. Robert couldn't resist any longer.

He got hard right away. Nancy unbuttoned his shirt and began to rub his chest with her hands. She placed one of her hands between his legs and rubbed his groin. She kissed his chest and sucked on his nipples. She unbuckled Robert's pants and let them fall to the floor. She rubbed his genitals inside his underwear and moaned. She pulled down Robert's underwear and watched him get harder. She switched back and forth from kissing his chest to his nipples. She teased and sucked on them as she moaned. Robert stood there, moaning and trembling, as she tasted him.

Suddenly Robert called out Nancy's name with pleasure. She stopped tasting him and, with her hand still on him, she pulled him down to the floor and on top of her. She whispered, "Put it in me, Robert, please put it in me." Robert grabbed himself and entered her. "Is it good, Robert? Is it good?" Nancy asked softly.

"Yes, it's good. It's so good I don't want to stop," he said. He began to stroke faster.

"I don't want you to stop. I don't want you to ever stop," she said loudly, as Robert came inside her. She hooked her legs around his body, and he kept moving up and down fast until she reached an orgasm. She hugged Robert, kissed him, and said, "I'm sorry, but I've fallen in love with you. I know that you still love Marie, but she's going to have to share you with me."

Robert didn't know what to say. He continued pumping her. Suddenly he felt a strong sensation. Robert moaned and came again. He was too tired to continue, so he lay beside Nancy on the floor to catch his breath. Nancy laid her head on Robert's chest, and they both fell asleep.

Marie came home from work and waited for Robert to call her. She decided to call him, but there was no answer. She sat on her couch thinking about Robert. She called again and again, but still there was no answer. She started to get nervous, so she decided to drive over to Robert's house to see if his car was in the yard. When she got there, she didn't see Robert's car, so she didn't get out. Marie decided to go back home and wait for him to call her. On the way home she got curious and decided to drive by Nancy's apartment to see if Robert's car was there. As Marie got closer to Nancy's apartment, she could see that Robert's car was parked in front of the apartment complex. Marie turned the car around and headed home. She began to cry uncontrollably. She couldn't see through her tears, so she pulled to the side of the road and stopped. She began to bang on the steering wheel with her fist as she cried and yelled, "I don't care. I just don't care anymore. Let him be with his other woman. I don't care!" In a few moments, Marie dried her eyes and began driving again.

I need a drink after all I've been through. I'm not going to drink much, and I don't think it will

affect my child, she thought. Marie pulled up to a bar, got out of the car, and went inside. She sat on a barstool and ordered a drink. She drank it down without hesitation. Then she drank another one and another. She sat there drinking until two o'clock in the morning.

When she got home, she went straight to bed. As she lay there, she thought of the way Robert made love to her. She wanted him, but he wasn't there. The thought of him aroused her to the point at which she was hot all over. She placed her hand on her breasts and began to pinch her nipples. Thinking of Robert, she began to rub her body. She placed her hands between her legs and rubbed her inner thighs until she started breathing rapidly. Her private parts became wet. She placed her middle finger inside herself and had an orgasm loudly. Marie turned onto her side, placed her hands between her knees, and fell asleep in moments.

Robert and Nancy slept through the night. When Nancy woke up, she saw that Robert was still asleep on the floor by her side. She reached down and felt his genitals as he slept.

At first there was no response, but Nancy kept feeling him until he began to get aroused. When Robert opened his eyes, Nancy took him into her mouth. He felt her hot, soft lips as she sucked him and got even harder. He placed his hands around Nancy's head and pushed her down until she had taken every inch of him.

When he came, he yelled, "Oh, Nancy!" He lay there on the floor feeling totally satisfied. It was as if Nancy had made him put everything he had into a release. He felt free. Nancy got up and went into the bathroom for a shower, while Robert lay on the floor thinking about how good she had made him feel. As he simmered down, he thought about the time. Then he remembered Marie. He thought of how he had planned to spend some time with her. He looked at the clock. It read nine o'clock. There was no window in Nancy's dining room, so Robert didn't know that it was nine o'clock the next morning. Robert got up and began to put on his clothes. He hoped it wasn't too late to call Marie.

Robert got dressed and yelled to Nancy in the shower, "I've got to go now. I'm leaving your key on the table."

When Robert walked out of the dining room, he noticed the light shining through the living room window. "I've really done it this time," he murmured. "Marie will never speak to me again."

Robert rushed to his car and drove home. When he arrived, he went inside and sat on his couch, trying to think of an excuse that would regain Marie's trust in him. He knew that she must have been disappointed when she couldn't reach him. Robert sat on his couch until he came to the conclusion that he would call Marie when she got home from work and ask her to come over to his house. He would make an excuse for not being home to receive her call the night before. Nancy had given him the best feeling he had ever had in his life, but he knew that his heart was for Marie, and he wanted her.

Robert kept busy during the rest of the day, but there was something that Nancy had told him that stayed in his mind. She told him that Marie would have to share him with her. Robert didn't agree with that. He thought if he and Marie got back together, there would be no cheating or sharing each other's love with someone else. *I'm going to have to call Nancy and talk to her about that and let her know that I'm not going to see her again.*

When Robert finished his work around the house, he went into the living room to relax for a few minutes because soon it would be time for Marie to get home from work. He decided that he was going to use the excuse that he went to a movie. Robert tried calling Marie every hour until eleven o'clock, but there was no answer. He finally gave up and went to bed.

He waited until after nine o'clock the next morning and then called Marie's office. They told him that Marie didn't come to work. Robert tried calling her at home, but still there was no answer.

One night after Robert had been trying to contact Marie for days, Nancy called Robert. She asked Robert why he hadn't called her lately.

Robert was angry that he wasn't able to get in touch with Marie, "Look," he said, "that was a bad stunt you pulled on me. I want you to know that I have no intentions of calling you again, and I would appreciate it if you didn't call me anymore either."

"You don't have to be so nasty about it. You can call me when you're feeling better," Nancy said.

Robert tried to tell her that he meant what he had said, but she hung up before he had the chance. Robert decided to see Marie at her house. If she wasn't home when he got there, he would wait until she came back. He got dressed and drove over to Marie's.

When he knocked on her door, Marie's mother answered. From her pleasant smile, Robert couldn't tell if she knew about the problems he and Marie were having. Marie's mother wasn't one to get in the middle of other's problems, especially not her daughter's, because Marie always got angry if her mother interfered or questioned her about her personal business. Since her husband had a stroke and was confined to bed, she had enough on her mind without collecting more trouble.

"Hi Robert, it's good to see you. Come in, sit down, make yourself comfortable," her mother said. She sat in a chair next to him. "I heard you've been in the hospital, but I take it you're all right now?"

"I'm doing fine now. It was just the flu," Robert said. "Is Marie home?

"No, she's not here right now," Marie's mother answered. "Do you mind if I wait for her?"

"Oh, no, I don't mind at all. While you're here, you may as well stay for supper. Marie normally calls me and lets me know where she is and when she's going to be back home, but she hasn't done that lately." She excused herself from the room and went into the kitchen to finish cooking the meal.

Robert stayed at Marie's house until ten thirty, but Marie still didn't come home. Robert thanked Marie's mother for a delicious supper and walked to the door to leave. Before leaving he said, "Please tell Marie I'll call her tomorrow."

"Okay, I'll let her know. Drive safe on your way home," said Marie's mother.

Chapter 10

Marie got home at midnight. She found her mother already asleep. Marie had been drinking a lot, and she was almost drunk when she got home. She went to her room and lay in her bed, but she had to get up because she was feeling sick. Marie rushed to the bathroom and vomited until there was nothing left in her stomach. Her eyes were bloodshot, and her lips dry. Her skin was cold, and she began to sweat profusely. Her skin trembled as if she was freezing. Marie made her way out of the bathroom to her mother's bedroom. She leaned against the door and knocked.

When her mother opened the door, Marie fell into her arms and said, "Mom, I'm sick." Her mother laid Marie on her bed, called the ambulance, and got a few things ready in case the medics took her to the hospital.

When the paramedics arrived, Marie's mother led them to Marie. The medics saw that Marie was breathing irregularly, so they put her on a stretcher and took her to the hospital. A team of doctors and nurses took her directly into the emergency room. The doctor checked her vital signs and gave her oxygen. Her mother had told the medics that Marie was expecting a child. When the doctor checked Marie, there was no second heartbeat. They put an IV in her arm, and performed a sonogram, but it was no use. Marie had miscarried. The doctor had smelled the alcohol on Marie's breath when she first came into the emergency room, so he ordered a blood test to check her blood alcohol level. It was high, and there were symptoms of alcohol poisoning. The doctor treated her for both the miscarriage and the alcohol poisoning and had her delivered to the emergency recovery room. Only time would tell how her recovery would progress.

Marie's mother arrived at the hospital shortly after and asked the nurse for information on her daughter. The nurse directed her to Marie's room and told her that she would get the doctor to speak to her about Marie's condition.

When her mother saw her daughter lying in the hospital bed with her eyes closed, she stroked Marie's forehead and began to cry. She said, "Oh, baby, what have you done to yourself?" She kissed Marie's cheeks. "You're going to be all right. God will take care of you."

Marie's mother dried her eyes when the doctor walked into the room. He extended his hand in greeting and said, "I'm Doctor Harris."

"I'm Mrs. Mason, Marie's mother."

"Well, Mrs. Mason, your daughter has had a miscarriage. At this time, we don't know what caused it. We've given her the necessary treatments and medications, and her vital signs are good, but she needs rest, and her body needs to heal. I ordered several tests to be done on Marie, which will take a little time. If these tests turn out okay, I see no reason why she can't go home. She'll be sleeping for a while because of the medication I've given her. At this point, that's all I can tell you until the test results come back. Do you have any questions?"

Marie's mother didn't have any, so Dr. Harris said good-bye and left the room. She sat at Marie's bedside and decided to let the rest of the family know that Marie was in the hospital. She didn't want to tell them that Marie had a miscarriage. She only told them that the doctor was keeping her in the hospital for a few days for observation.

Nancy called Robert morning and night for two days. Whenever Robert saw her number come up on the caller ID, he wouldn't answer the phone. Robert was still upset that he couldn't get in touch with Marie. On the third day when she called, he decided it was time to answer the phone.

"I called to say that I'm sorry for what happened when you came to return my key," Nancy started. "And most of all, I'm sorry for telling you I'm in love with you. Maybe if I hadn't done those things, we'd still be friends and talking. I guess you could say I needed someone at the time, and you were so sweet to me, I couldn't help but fall in love with you. For that, I'm sorry. Not for feeling what I felt with you, but for telling you about it. I had no intentions of damaging our friendship."

“Well,” said Robert, “I’m sorry, too, because I’ve been treating you coldly. I should be thanking you for making me feel better than I’ve ever felt in my life. Would you be willing to let bygones be bygones?”

“Sure, you’re forgiven, and if there’s ever anything I can help you with, just let me know.”

“The same goes for me,” Robert said.

“Okay, then. I’ve got to get busy now, but I had to tell you I was sorry. I’ll be talking with you. Good-bye.”

In the middle of the night, while Marie lay sleeping in her hospital bed, she called out Robert’s name. The nurse heard her and the next morning asked Marie’s mother if she knew someone named Robert.

“That’s my son-in-law,” Mrs. Mason said.

“She must have been dreaming about him,” the nurse said and went back to her station.

Mrs. Mason found a pay phone and called Robert. “Hello, Robert, this is Mrs. Mason.”

“Oh, yes. How are you?”

“Oh, I’m not feeling so good,” said Mrs. Mason, her voice trembling. “What’s wrong?” Robert asked.

“Well,” said Mrs. Mason, “when Marie came home a few nights ago, she got sick, and I called the ambulance to take her to the hospital. She’s still here now. Through all the excitement I almost forgot to call you. I’m sorry it took me so long to call.” She burst into tears.

“Don’t cry, and don’t worry, I’ll be there in a few minutes. I’ll talk to you when I get there, okay?”

“Okay,” Mrs. Mason said, still sobbing. After Robert hung up the telephone, he rushed to his car and drove to the hospital. When he arrived, he went to the information desk to get Marie’s room number and her doctor’s name. He found Marie’s mother there in Marie’s room.

Robert walked over to the bed where Marie lay. He looked at her and smiled at her sleeping. He looked at the oxygen tube and the IV that was connected to her. His face paled, and he sat in the chair at her bedside.

“What happened to her?” Robert asked.

“I don’t understand all the details, but the doctor can explain them to you. I’m just too nervous to explain anything,” Mrs. Mason said.

Robert got up and went down the hallway to the nurse’s station. “Excuse me, is Dr. Harris

in?"

"Yes," said the nurse," but he's busy with a patient right now. Is there something I might be able to help you with?"

"No, I don't think so," said Robert. "I wanted to speak to Dr. Harris about my wife's condition."

"What's your wife's name?" asked the nurse. "Marie Maxwell."

"Oh, you must be Robert. Your wife was calling your name in her sleep. As soon as the doctor is finished with his patient, I'll send him in to talk to you."

"Okay," said Robert, "thank you very much." He walked back to Marie's room and sat by her bedside.

A little while later, the doctor came in. He said hello to Marie's mother and greeted Robert with a handshake. "Marie had a miscarriage," the doctor said, "and at this point, we don't know the cause. Her vital signs are good, and the reason that she's still asleep is because of the medication we've been giving her. When she came to the emergency room, she was dehydrated and had an alcohol blood count of point twenty, meaning that she'd been drinking quite a bit. We're holding her here until other tests are confirmed. Is there anything that we can do or get for you to make your visit here more comfortable?"

"Do you think Marie will be here for a very long time?" Robert asked. "Well, after we get the test results back, and if they're all okay, we should be able to release her in a few more days."

"Thank you," said Robert.

The doctor said good day to Mrs. Mason and told Robert that it was nice meeting him and if he thought of anything else he needed to ask, to let him know. The doctor left the room.

"Well, I'm going to go find the cafeteria so I can get something to eat. Would you like something?" asked Robert.

"Oh, no, thank you. I ate just before you came," Mrs. Mason said. Robert walked out of the room and down the hallway, looking for the cafeteria.
He really wasn't hungry. He just wanted to be alone so he could get a grip on this new information. When he reached the nurses' station, he asked one of the nurses for directions. She told him it was down another floor, so he walked to the stairwell. Suddenly, what Dr. Harris had said about Marie's condition and the alcohol content in her blood hit him. Robert stopped walking and sat on a stair. He realized that Marie wasn't going to have his child, and he began to cry. He thought *why did she break her promise to me? She told me she wouldn't take another drink until our child was born.*

When his sobs passed, Robert got up and continued down the stairs to the cafeteria. He realized he didn't have an appetite so he got a soda and sat in one of the plastic chairs. He thought of the problems that he and Marie were having. Most upsetting to him was the thought that the miscarriage was caused by Marie's drinking. Robert thought maybe it happened for the best. There was a possibility that if she had the child, it would have been damaged physically or mentally.

Robert came to the conclusion that he would do all that he could to help Marie get back on her feet, but then he would tell her that he could not deal with her drinking problems, and if she continued, he would leave her. His thoughts were so disordered that he forgot that he and Marie weren't together and he didn't have the right to tell her anything. She didn't have to see him if she didn't want to.

Marie opened her eyes and looked around the room. She looked over and saw her mother asleep in a chair. As Marie's mind cleared, she wondered why she was in the hospital. The only thing that she remembered was that she got off from work and stopped at a bar. Very softly she called to her mother until she woke up. Her mother squeezed Marie's hand and said, "Thank God you're awake. How do you feel, sweetheart?"

"I feel fine. What happened to me?" Marie asked. She wasn't having any pain, and she didn't feel as if she had any serious injuries.

"Don't you remember getting sick at home?" her mother asked. "No."

"Well, you got sick, and the ambulance had to pick you up and take you to the hospital. Don't you feel anything?"

"No, should I?" Then Marie thought about her pregnancy, and she asked her mother about the baby. Her mother told her that she had a miscarriage. Marie couldn't hold back the tears and started screaming, "Oh, no! Mom, no." Her mother tried to comfort her. When that didn't work, she pushed the call button.

The nurse ran to the room and saw Marie's mother holding Marie in her arms, trying to get her to calm down.

"I'll give her something to settle her down a bit." The nurse rushed out and then returned with a syringe.

She put the needle in Marie's arm and explained, "This will start working in about two minutes. You may feel weak, but don't worry. It's only going to make you rest."

When Marie began to calm down, her mother sat by her bedside and held her hand. "Don't worry, my child. Everything's going to be just fine." The tremor in her voice didn't match her words, but like mothers have always done, she tried to put up a brave image for the sake of her daughter.

Soon Marie was feeling calm. She said, "Don't tell Robert about the miscarriage because I want to talk to him first."

"Sweetheart, Robert already knows about the miscarriage. He's down in the cafeteria getting something to eat. He should be back shortly. When the doctor told him everything, he took it well."

"Did the doctor say why I had the miscarriage?" Marie asked. "Wait. Never mind that right now. Mom, please, when Robert comes back, tell him that I don't want to see anyone right now, and I'll call him later."

"Why do you want me to tell him that? Aren't you two getting along?" "You know we're separated,

Mom."

"Well, if you ask me, that doesn't mean anything because you see each other all the time. Why, Robert was just over at the house looking for you the night you got sick. He stayed for supper. I intended to tell you about it, but, well, you know. I'm sorry if I caused a problem for you two."

"Oh, no," said Marie, "I'm just not ready to face him yet."

When Robert came back to Marie's room, her mother met him at the door. "Let's take a walk to the dayroom. I need to talk to you for a minute," Mrs. Mason told him.

While they sat in the dayroom, Marie's mother told Robert that Marie wasn't feeling well and that she was not in the mood to see anyone. "Marie will give you a call when she's feeling better."

Robert said, "Would you tell her that if there's anything I can do to help, just let me know? She's got my number, so don't hesitate to call."

"Thank you very much," said Mrs. Mason. "I'll tell her that." Robert got up and said, "I guess I'll go home then and get some work done. I'll see you later."

By the time Mrs. Mason returned to Marie's room, Marie had fallen asleep. When she woke up, she saw that her mother had fallen asleep again. Marie lay there trying to think what she would do and where she would go next. There was one thing she thought for sure. She wasn't going to get back together with Robert, not after he had been sleeping with Nancy.

Marie began to pray and asked God to forgive her if she had caused the loss of her child by drinking and to help her get back on her feet. Three days passed, and Marie got stronger each day. She had started to do things for herself, like use the restroom, sit up in her bed, and comb her hair.

The doctor came into Marie's room and said, "Well, Mrs. Maxwell, it looks like you're feeling better today."

"I am," said Marie. "I'm feeling much better." She asked the doctor if he knew what had caused her to have a miscarriage.

The doctor told her that it was probably caused from the lack of nourishment needed to maintain the fetus. He said there was no reason to think she couldn't get pregnant again and carry a child full term. "Since your entire test results were okay, I see no reason to keep you here any longer. I've written some prescriptions that I want you to take until you visit my office on the fifteenth of next month. When you get the medications, take them as directed, and you shouldn't have any problems. In the event that you do have problems, you need to check into the hospital immediately, and someone will contact me. When you're ready to leave, pass by the nurses' station and pick up your discharge papers."

The doctor wished Marie well and left. Marie's mother began to prepare her things. The nurse rolled her to the exit door in a wheelchair. Marie got out, climbed into her mother's car, and they rode home.

When Marie walked into the house, she said, "Thank God, I'm home again." "Now, Marie," her mother said, "I don't think you should try to get back into the swing of things too quickly. You should just stay here in the house today and rest."

"I know you want what's best for me, Mom, but don't you think I rested enough while I was in the hospital? I need to go to the drugstore to get my prescriptions filled."

"Now don't you go telling me what you need to do," said Mrs. Mason. "I'll go to the drugstore and get the prescriptions for you." As Marie fussed, her mother said, "I don't think you should be driving around by yourself yet."

Marie smiled at her mother and said, "Okay, Mom. I'll do some straightening up while you go. How's that?"

"Oh no, don't you do anything. Just sit down and rest. I can straighten things up when I get back."

"Okay, you win. I'll just go to my room and lie down."

When Marie was alone in the house, she realized how much she had wanted to have her child. Now she would have to face the reality that there would be no child. She thought of the things that had happened between her and Robert and decided that she would never get back together with him. She knew that she must get on with her life and try to leave her past behind her. Marie also knew that she would have to talk to Robert sooner or later to let him know about her decision to not get back together with him. All Marie wanted was to try to piece her life back together.

When her mother returned from the drugstore, she saw that Marie was looking sad.

"Are you feeling okay?" her mother asked. "Yeah," said Marie, "I guess so."

"Well," said Mrs. Mason, "don't worry about anything. Things are going to work out just fine, you'll see."

Chapter 11

Months passed, and Robert and Marie still hadn't talked to each other. Marie had fully recovered. Although she still drank, she drank moderately. She put herself and her happiness first. She began taking advantage of every situation that would benefit her. She would go to any extent to get what she wanted. Her job became the most important part of her life. She got a new job as a social worker's assistant. She processed and filed reports that were sent into the office from caseworkers in the field. Marie was smart, and success was at hand. She kept copies of the reports that she turned in and memorized them for future reference. Whenever the caseworkers met with the supervisors to discuss issues, they would ask for clarification from previous reports. Marie would save the day by giving them direct answers to their questions and help them identify particular reports to research in order to support her answers.

One day when Marie was taking a break at work, she saw a gentleman that reminded her of Robert. She started to think of Robert and wonder what happened to him, but she pushed the thoughts away. She had just started to enjoy life a little and didn't want to let anyone interfere with that. She wanted love and affection, but it would just have to take a back seat to her material needs.

Marie's supervisor was a beautiful and intelligent young woman named Linda. Marie was

constantly getting good comments from the "higher ups," and Linda had been paying close attention to Marie's work performance.

One day Linda called Marie into her office. Marie wondered if she had done something wrong and was nervous when she walked through the door. Linda told her to relax.

"I just want you to have lunch with me today," Linda said.

Marie felt a sense of relief and said, "Okay, I'll get my purse." Marie went back to her office with a smile on her face. When she returned, she and Linda got into the company car. Linda took Marie to a cozy little restaurant. While they waited for a waitress, Marie said, "I wish they'd hurry up and wait on us. I only have thirty minutes for lunch. By the time I get back, I'm going to be late."

Linda looked at Marie and smiled. "Let me worry about that. Did you forget I'm your supervisor?"

Marie laughed and said, "Okay, thanks."

They talked about their jobs and other mundane things. Marie felt Linda looking into her soul as she talked. She started to get uncomfortable talking with Linda, but she wondered if she was just seeing things that weren't there.

Linda invited Marie out to lunch every day. They enjoyed each other's company and became close friends. One day at lunch, Linda got on to the subject of men.

"I can't stand them," Linda said frowning. "They're always trying to take advantage of a woman's love. They treat you nice for a while, and then all of a sudden they change." Linda got Marie to talk about her past. Tears began to well in Marie's eyes.

Linda said, "You don't have to say anymore; I understand just how you feel. Why do we need men in our lives anyway? They never cause anything but heartache and pain."

She reached over and stroked Marie's chin with her finger, saying, "I really understand what you've been through, but you don't have to worry anymore. Just hold your head up high because I'll be there for you when you need me."

They became such close friends that they didn't keep secrets from each other. They planned to go to a concert, but Linda phoned ahead of time and said her car wasn't working. She asked Marie to pick her up at her apartment so they could drive to the concert together. When Marie arrived, Linda asked her to sit down for a drink.

The apartment was cozy, and Linda had music playing softly. She handed Marie a strong drink and sat on the couch beside her. They laughed and talked as they drank. Time passed and Linda said, "Oh, my, look what time it is! We can't make the concert now. By the time we get there, it'll be half over."

"That's all right," said Marie. "We can always catch a concert another day." "Okay, then. Let's have another drink."

After a few drinks, Linda began to question Marie about her sex life. Marie told Linda that it had been a while since she had sex with anyone. As a matter of fact, it had been months since she had had sex. She said that she had not found a person that she trusted enough to have sex with.

"What kind of person would you be interested in?" Linda asked. "Well," said Marie, "someone who wants me for more than just sex, and someone who's not going to try to change me into something that I'm not."

"How do you feel about having sex with a woman?"

Marie laughed and said, "The way I feel now I could have sex with anything that walked." They both laughed, and they looked deep into each other's eyes. The laughter stopped when Linda reached out and gently stroked Marie's hair.

"Your hair is beautiful. You're beautiful," Linda whispered. Linda held the back of Marie's head and pulled her close for a kiss. Marie was intoxicated but realized what was going on. Marie pushed her away, saying, "What are you doing?"

Linda said, "I'm sorry. I just got carried away." Marie staggered away from the couch. She threw the glass on the floor and swayed out of Linda's apartment. Marie sat in her car until she sobered up a little. When Marie got home, she went straight to bed and fell asleep. The next morning Marie remembered the incident and didn't want to see Linda, so she called in sick. Later that day, the phone rang and Marie answered.

"Hello, may I speak to Marie?"

"This is she," Marie said.

"This is Linda. I want to apologize to you for what happened last night. I just lost control of myself."

Marie remembered how she got out of control while drinking and the trouble she had always caused herself. "Go on. I'm listening."

"I value our friendship, and I feel closer to you than I do to my own blood," Linda said. "I know I should have told you that I was a lesbian, but I didn't want to lose your friendship. My own family doesn't accept me because of the way I am, but they seem to forget that I didn't make myself. I needed someone to talk to, and I thought that person was you because I felt that you understood me."

Marie felt sorry for Linda and said, "I understand everything that we talked about, but if you wanted me to be your friend, then you should have told me that you were gay and at least given me the choice of whether I wanted to be friends or not. We've known each other for some time now, and I put a lot of trust into our friendship. You disappointed me when you acted like a pig and tried to steal what you wanted from me."

"Was it that bad?" asked Linda.

"No, it wasn't that bad," said Marie. "It was the fact that you didn't tell me that you were a lesbian, and I shared all of my secrets with you."

"I was going to tell you," said Linda, "but I was trying to pick the right time when you could understand me better. I'd give anything to make things the way they were with us, but sooner or later, you would have found out or heard a rumor about me. Then things would have been worse than they are now. Can you forgive me?"

Marie thought for a few minutes and said, "Well, I think it's best if we just leave our friendship at the office."

"Okay," said Linda, "I understand."

When Marie got off the phone, she paused for a few minutes. She thought maybe she was being a little hard on Linda. After all, she had been a good friend, and they had fun times together. Then Marie's thoughts turned around. *If I don't have anything to do with Linda outside work, will she try to get back at me by getting me in trouble?*

Marie had applied for a supervisor position in the same building. Linda was Marie's supervisor and could give Marie the job evaluation that she needed to get the position. This was the new Marie, and she was driven to get what she wanted, regardless of relationships. Marie decided to string her along as a friend until she got the position she wanted. Then she would dump Linda.

The next morning on her desk, Marie found a dozen red roses and a card from Linda, which read, "Please accept my apologies." At first, Marie didn't know what to do or say. Marie thought the roses were beautiful, but the idea of who sent them, and why, was sickening to her. She threw the roses into the trashcan. Then she remembered her plan to string Linda on and took the roses out of the trash and placed them on her desk. She would throw them away on her way home that evening instead.

Marie called Linda and thanked her for the roses. "Linda, the roses were beautiful. I accept your apology."

"Thanks," Linda said. "You made my day. Would you like to have lunch?" Marie hesitated before she answered. She almost said no but when she thought about her plan, she said, "Sure, what time?"

"I'll pick you up at noon."

For the next two months, their friendship went well. Linda received a form from the manager's office along with a memo asking her to evaluate Marie's work performance. As a supervisor, she often got this request and thought nothing of it. She gave Marie the highest score that a worker could get and sent the form back to the manager's office.

Marie had been selected for the position of supervisor, and as far as management was concerned, Marie had the job if she wanted it. All that was left to do was to ask her to accept the position and have her move into her new office.

The next day, Linda received a memo to have Marie report to the main office at nine o'clock. Linda faxed Marie a memo giving her instructions on what to do and where to go. When Linda discovered that Marie was being transferred with a promotion, she went to her boss and asked if they could raise Marie's salary to match that of the transfer salary. She hoped that Marie would change her mind about being transferred.

Marie went to the main building and knocked on the office door. She heard a voice say the door was open. She walked into the room, and one of the managers said, "You must be Marie."

"Yes," said Marie, and she handed him the memo. "Well, have a seat, Mrs. Maxwell," the manager

said.

Marie sat down and listened as the manager explained why she was asked to come to that office. "Your application was accepted for the position of supervisor. Out of twenty-five applicants, we found that you're the most qualified for the job. We've also decided that an interview for this position is not necessary since the job posting was internal, so we called you over to ask you if you wanted the position."

"Oh, yes, very much so. Thank you."

"Well then, I see no reason to keep you here any longer. You will probably want to pack up your office to get ready to transfer here tomorrow. Your current supervisor and manager have already been informed of the transfer, so just report to this office tomorrow morning at nine o'clock for your supervisors' orientation."

Marie got up with a smile on her face, and she smiled all the way back to her old office.

She began to get her things together from her desk. Just as Marie finished packing her boxes and was getting ready to leave, the phone rang. "Hello," said Linda. "I have some news for you. I checked with my bosses, and they said they'd raise your salary to match a supervisor's pay if you stay with us."

Marie was in a hurry to leave, so she asked, "How long do I have before I have to give them an answer?"

"Well," said Linda, "just send them a memo in the morning. I have to go now. Someone is on the other line. I'll talk to you after work."

Marie grabbed her things, left the building, and headed for home. Later that day, management got in touch with Linda and told her that she would have a new employee coming in the morning to replace Marie. Linda was surprised because she didn't know Marie had been officially transferred. She thought, *Marie didn't even say anything to me about getting a new job. I wonder why?* Linda wasn't sure what was going on with Marie. She dialed her office, but there was no answer. She walked down to Marie's office to ask her about the transfer. When Linda opened the door, she found that the office was empty.

On her way home, Linda decided to call Marie at her house and try to find out what was going on. When Marie's mother answered the phone, she was informed that Marie wasn't home.

At ten-thirty, and after two bottles of wine, which she drank while worrying about her best friend, she called Marie again. This time Marie answered. "Marie, this is Linda. I'm trying to find out what happened to you today. No one told me anything, and my boss tells me I have a new employee to break in tomorrow. Does that mean you took the other job?"

"Yes, and I'm happy with my decision," Marie said matter-of-factly.

"Well, you could have let me know. After all, we're friends aren't we?" "Friends?" Marie said. "Honey, you're no friend of mine. As a matter of fact, I don't like you, and I can't stand being around you."

Linda began to cry. "Why are you trying to hurt me? What did I do to deserve this? I don't understand. I love you!" Marie hung up without another word.

Marie was doing well on her new job. There were two of her co-workers who would whisper to each other and laugh when Marie was seen walking down the hall or in the cafeteria, and it bothered her. One day she decided to confront them. At lunch, instead of dining by herself, Marie went to the table where her co-workers were sitting. "Hi, my name's Marie. May I sit with you?"

They looked at each other, and one of them said, "Why not? Be our guest." Marie set her tray on the table and took a seat.

"My name is Ann, and this is Jean," said Ann.

"Nice meeting the both of you," said Marie. As they began to eat, Marie said, "I'm not one to beat around the bush, so I hope that you don't get offended by what I'm about to ask you. Why is it that whenever you see me, you always laugh and whisper? I'm beginning to wonder if I dress funny or look funny to you."

Ann said, "No, honey, you're not funny, but she is." "Now just what is that supposed to mean?"

"A person is sometimes judged by the company she keeps," Ann said, smirking. "Can you be a little more specific?" Marie asked, starting to get aggravated by these two.

Ann said, "Taylor's Hall."

The only thing Marie could think of was that she had been there once with Linda to a concert. Marie put it all together. "You think I'm a lesbian because you saw me with Linda at Taylor's Hall?"

"Well, sometimes people are judged by the company they keep," Ann repeated. Marie was beginning to get angry. She said, "Although the company I keep is none of your business, I'll have you know that I'm not a lesbian. Linda was my supervisor before I got this promotion. Just for the record, I'd appreciate it if you would keep your implications to yourself." Marie got up from the table and said, "Good day, ladies. I seem to have lost my appetite." She walked out of the cafeteria and returned to her office. Marie sat in her chair behind her desk and began to wonder if there were other people who had seen her and Linda together and thought they were lovers. There was nothing that Marie could do about that now. *I need a man in my life, and then maybe people will see that I'm straight,* Marie thought.

The next day at lunch, Marie went to the cafeteria. She sat at a table by herself. Ann and Jean came over to the table and asked, "May we eat lunch with you today?"

Marie looked up at them and said, "Sure, if you don't mind eating with someone that you think is a lesbian."

Ann and Jean sat at the table. Ann said, "We want to apologize for our judgment of you and the way we acted in the hallway and at lunch yesterday. Like you said, it's your business who your friends are. I've always considered myself to be a fair woman. I'm honest and truthful, and I don't mind saying what's on my mind. Being a woman myself, I can't see women running around sleeping with each other. It reflects on me as a woman. If it continues, before long, men will have to find out if you're a lesbian before they appreciate your feminine qualities."

"Well," said Marie, "I don't think women should be running around having sex with each other either. It's disgusting to me as well, but I do think that people should be allowed to live as

they choose without being ridiculed."

"You're not the kind of person who's afraid to speak up for what you believe in and express your views," said Ann. "You're pretty much like me in that way."

Marie smiled and said, "Watch it with that 'like me' stuff, or it won't be long before somebody's saying we're going with each other." They all laughed and enjoyed their lunch.

Marie got along well with her co-workers after that day. She became close friends with a few, but she never let anyone get too close. One evening, Marie and some of her co-workers decided to get together for a meeting to discuss an upcoming Christmas party. When the meeting was over, a few decided to stop at Jake's Lounge for a few drinks before going home, and Marie was included. They were sitting in the lounge, drinking and talking, when a handsome man walked into the bar. All the ladies at the table saw him and began to make comments on his appearance.

Ann said, "Careful ladies. Everyone at this table is married except Marie." One of the women said, "He's fine, but not as fine as my husband." They began to chatter about their husbands.

"Well, Marie," said Ann, "you're the only one sitting here who hasn't said anything. What do you think about him?"

"Well, he does look nice, and he's probably got three or more women already, but I wouldn't mind taking him on." The guy was tall and had muscles like Mr. Universe. He wore a beige, double-breasted suit and a diamond on his finger that glittered when he moved his hand. Everyone at the table laughed as they said, "Go for it, Marie. Go for it." Marie excused herself from the table and went into the ladies' room. When she came out, she walked to the bar and sat in the seat next to the man. Marie wanted to see if the guy would introduce himself, which would mean that he was interested. She sat there as if she was waiting for the bartender to bring her a drink. When the guy turned and looked at her, he said, "Excuse me, my name's Baron. Can I get you something to drink?"

Marie's face tingled as she smiled and said, "Thanks, I'll have a rum and coke." Baron called the bartender over and asked him to bring a rum and coke for Marie. Then he said, "I didn't catch your name."

"Oh, I'm sorry." She held her hand out. "Marie Maxwell."

Baron took her hand and held it. "It's a pleasure to be in the company of such a beautiful woman."

"Why, thank you. It's not every day I get such a delightful compliment." They toasted each other and sat at the bar getting to know each other better. When Marie looked over toward the table, she saw Ann point her finger toward the ladies' room. Marie excused herself from the bar and went into the ladies' room. Ann followed shortly after.

Chapter 12

"Oh, Marie, honey, looks like you struck the mother load," Ann said, laughing. "Listen, we're getting ready to leave. We won't disturb you and your company, so don't waste time saying goodnight to us. Just hang in there, and don't let that man get away from you. See you tomorrow at

lunch." Ann walked out of the ladies' room and back to the table. When Marie came out, Ann and her co-workers were leaving. Marie returned to the bar and sat next to Baron.

"You know, tonight must be my lucky night," Baron said. "Why is that?" asked Marie.

"Because I've been coming here now for quite some time, and tonight's the first night I've met a woman that I really wanted to talk with."

"Oh, really?" Marie asked.

"Yes, really. Most women I've met here either didn't want to be bothered, or they were married and looking for someone on the side. But I try to stay away from those types because I don't want to get hurt, nor do I want to be in jail."

"Why would you be in jail?" Marie asked.

"Well, you can't see a married woman when you want to; you have to see her when you can. And if you fall in love with her, you can't have her to yourself. That causes you to get all bottled-up inside and be confined to just waiting around for the moment when you can be with the one that you love. To me, that's like being locked up in jail."

"Yes, I guess you're right. No one should be in that position." "Are you married?" Baron asked.

"Yes, but I've been separated from my husband for almost a year now." "Why don't you get a divorce?" Baron inquired.

"When my husband and I separated, I went through some hard changes. I didn't want to accept the fact that we weren't going to get back together. He wanted to get an uncontested divorce, but at the time I wouldn't sign the papers. Then, when I was sure that we weren't going to reunite, I never saw him again to mention the divorce."

"Did you have any kids?" Baron probed.

Marie wanted to tell him that she had a miscarriage, but the thought made her too emotional. She said, "No, no kids."

"Well," said Baron, "at least you don't have to worry about a kid growing up without a father."

"Are you married?" asked Marie.

"Been there, done that, and it didn't work out," said Baron. "Any kids?"

"I have a son that I supported until he became an adult. Now he's on his own in the Air Force, and thank God for that. There's just too much trouble in the streets these days to have to raise a child in the city. I'm thankful that I was able to keep my son under control until he was able to get out on his own."

"At least you aren't one of those fathers that ran out on his child because he and the mother couldn't get along," said Marie. "But I guess we have to live with the cards that life deals us. Then we have to play the hand the best way we know how."

"You're exactly right," Baron said, smiling.

At closing time, Baron asked Marie if she needed a ride home. Marie told him that she had her car.

"Well then," said Baron, "do you mind if I walk with you to your car?" "Okay, but first I must go to the ladies' room," Marie said.

When she came back, they left the lounge together. At Marie's car, Baron asked her, "Do you suppose I could call you sometime for an evening out on the town?"

"What did you have in mind?" Marie asked.

"There's a concert starring Michael Jackson at the arena Saturday night. Would you like to go?"

"Oh, sure" said Marie. "I love Michael's music."

"Well then," Baron said, "if you give me your phone number, I'll call you tomorrow and give you the details."

She gave him her number and said, "Thanks for a wonderful evening." "It was my pleasure," Baron said.

The next day when Marie went to work, she stayed busy for about an hour. She was thinking about the moment when Baron had asked her why she didn't get a divorce. The more she thought about it, the more she knew that it was the best thing for her to do. She called the attorney's office and made an appointment for that same evening to find out how to file for the divorce. Marie planned to work through her lunch hour to make up the time she missed leaving early. When lunchtime came, she didn't leave her office.

Ann and Jean waited about twenty minutes in the cafeteria. When Marie didn't show up, Ann got impatient and said, "Well, you know what they say, if Mohammed won't come to the mountain, then the mountain must go to Mohammed." They laughed. She said, "I'm going to walk down to Marie's office to see if she's here today. Are you coming?"

"Yes, I wouldn't miss this for anything."

They walked down the hallway to Marie's office, and Ann knocked on the door. "It's open," Marie said.

Ann pushed the door open and said, "What's this? Are you trying to ignore us today after a fantastic night with Romeo himself?"

"No," said Marie, laughing. "I want to take off early today, so I'm working through my lunch hour."

"Well," said Ann, "in that case, I guess it's all right. But tomorrow you've got to tell us what happened with you and Romeo."

"Well, I can tell you now. We just talked a little and got to know each other, and his name isn't Romeo. It's Baron. Anyway, he walked me to my car, and I drove home alone."

"Are you sure you're not leaving something out?"

"Okay," said Marie, "if you must know, Baron asked me out to the Michael Jackson concert on Saturday night at the arena."

"Good," Ann said. She gave Marie a hug and said, "I hope you two have a wonderful time. I'm so happy for you. Well, now that we know your business, we'll leave you alone and let you get your work done while we go down to the cafeteria and spread the news about you and Baron."

As they walked toward the door, Ann turned and asked, "You don't mind us spreading your business, do you?"

"Of course not," Marie said. She laughed and said, "Get out of here." Ann and Jean left, and Marie spent the rest of the day thinking about Baron and what she was going to wear Saturday night. After work, she stopped at the lawyer's office.

The lawyer told Marie about the no-fault divorce and said he would do the paperwork and have it ready for her Tuesday.

"I'll contact Robert and have him sign the divorce papers. If he signs, the divorce will be in effect in sixty days."

Marie went home and waited for Baron to call her and tell her the details for Saturday night. Marie didn't go to bed until midnight, and still Baron didn't call. Marie finally fell asleep.

The next morning when Marie woke up, she was angry. Her first thought was not to go to work. Marie knew that Ann and Jean would be questioning her about Baron, and she was in no mood for that. Marie began to think about her past and how she used to be weak enough to let things get in her way. She thought *I'm going to work. Baron doesn't have to call me if he doesn't want to. We're not obligated to each other or anything. Oh well, he was too good to be true, anyway.* Marie went to work prepared to tell Ann and Jean the bad news about Baron. Driving to work, she said aloud, stating a fact as much as trying to convince herself, "I won't let a man bring me down again."

Marie thought about what an old friend of hers had said long ago: *You reap what you sow.* Marie remembered the time when she led Linda to believe that she was her friend but was only stringing her along to get a good job rating. After all the things that Marie had been through, she was still clinging to despair, but she was going to survive, and she would use any advantage that she could to get what she wanted.

Marie walked into work with a smile on her face and not a negative thought on her mind. It was easier now for Marie to get over disappointments after being disappointed so many times before. She decided to chalk all of her disappointments up to another round of experience.

When Ann saw Marie smiling at lunchtime, she said, "Okay Marie, what did Baron do last night to have you smiling today?"

"Oh no, the smile isn't from Baron. That creep didn't say anything. He promised to call me last night and give me the details on the concert Saturday night, but the asshole didn't call."

After lunch, Marie returned to her office and worked happily for the rest of the day. When Marie got home, she saw a dozen roses in a vase on the table. "Mom!" she yelled, "Who are the

flowers for?"

Her mother came into the living room and said, "They're for you, dear. Open the card so we can see who sent them."

Marie smiled and said, "What do you mean we?"

Her mother said, "Okay, if you don't want me to know, I'll just go into the other room."

"Don't be hurt. I was only kidding. It looks as if you already opened the card anyway," Marie said, laughing.

When Marie looked at the card, she saw that the roses where from Baron. "Is Baron one of your new boyfriends?" asked Marie's mother. "See, Mom? I told you that you already looked at my card. How else would you know this card was from Baron?"

Her mother said, "I'm sorry, sweetheart, but when I saw those beautiful roses, I just couldn't resist the temptation. I peeked at the card, but it won't happen again. I promise."

Marie kissed her mom on the cheek and said, "That's okay." On the card, Baron apologized for not calling. He wrote that he would call her tomorrow night at eight.

"Well," said Marie, "it's no big deal." She put the roses and the vase on the table in the living room and went about the house doing her normal after-work chores. Marie read and watched television until seven thirty. Then she began to wonder if Baron was going to call at eight o'clock like he had said he would. While she was wondering, the doorbell rang. "I'll get it, Mom."

She walked toward the front door and opened it. Marie was surprised to see Baron standing there. She was nervous because she was wearing her housecoat and a scarf tied around her head to keep the dust out of her hair while she was cleaning. She didn't think she was dressed for the occasion. She was in a daze, as he stood in the doorway.

"Hello, Marie," Baron said. "I hope I'm not disturbing you, but since I owe you an apology, I decided I should do it in person. May I come in?"

"Oh yes. Please excuse my bad manners, but you know how it is when you're not expecting company. Have a seat and make yourself comfortable. I'll be with you in a moment." Marie, slightly embarrassed, rushed out to make herself more presentable. When she came out, she asked Baron if she could get him a drink.

"Sure, I'll have a soda, please."

Marie went into the kitchen. Her mother walked through the hallway, looked into the living room, and saw Baron sitting on the couch. She walked into the living room and said, "You must be Baron."

Baron stood up to shake her hand, and, bowing, said, "I'm Baron. It's a pleasure to meet you. Are you Marie's sister?"

"Don't even try it," she said. "I'm Marie's mother, Mrs. Mason, and you know

it."

"Oh, no. You look young enough to be her sister." "Yes, I know, her older sister maybe," she said laughing. Marie walked into the living room and said, "Oh, Mom, this is Baron." "Never mind," said her mother, "I've already met Baron, so I'll go finish my work and leave you two alone. Nice meeting you, Baron, and the flowers were beautiful."

Marie passed Baron his soda. They sat and talked and talked on the couch, and before they knew it, it was eleven thirty.

"Well," said Marie, "I don't know about you, but it's getting late, and I have to go to work in the morning. There's still something I need to get done before turning in for the night."

Baron stood up and said, "It's been a pleasure visiting you, and I hope you'll have me back again sometime soon."

"I enjoyed talking to you, too," said Marie.

Baron stopped suddenly on the way to the front door and said, "Oh, I almost forgot. Is your mother still awake? I want to say goodnight to her before I leave."

"She's either reading or asleep, but if she's still awake, I'll tell her that you said goodnight."

"Good. I hope to see more of her in the future." Baron opened the door and then he turned, took Marie's hand in his, and raised it to his lips. He looked into her eyes and kissed her hand. He said, "This is goodnight, until we meet again."

Baron got in his car and waved to Marie as he pulled away. Marie slowly watched him drive away before closing the door. She shook her head to snap herself back to reality. She thought *He probably won't be back again anyway.*

Marie went to the cafeteria the next day. As usual, Ann and Jean were there, so Marie got her food and went over to the table where they were sitting.

"Hello, ladies," said Marie.

"Hi, Marie," they said as Marie sat down.

Ann asked, "What's the scoop on Baron? Aren't you going to call him and ask him why he lied to you about calling you the other night?"

She answered, "Oh, he made up for it by sending me a dozen roses." "Oh, really? That sounds serious enough for me," said Ann. "Oh, its no big deal. He probably sends flowers to all his girlfriends." "Flowers, yes, but roses? Honey, I think the man's serious." "That's right. I married the man that sent me roses," Jean stated. They all laughed as they enjoyed their meal. When Marie got home from work, she noticed that there was a message on her answering machine. The caller was Baron. "Hello Marie, Baron here. A new movie is showing at the theater downtown tonight at eight. I'll be by for you about seven thirty. See you then."

Marie took a deep breath and thought; *He didn't even ask me if I wanted to go. Do I want to go?* She answered her own question by rushing to prepare herself for her date.

Mrs. Mason came into the room and said, "My, my, you're really moving fast. That guy

Baron is coming over tonight, isn't he?"

"Yes," said Marie. "Baron is coming over, but not for a visit. We're going to see a movie tonight. By the way, Baron told me to tell you goodnight last night, if you were still awake. But you weren't, so I didn't want to wake you up."

"That was sweet of him."

They talked about the movie Marie and Baron were planning to see. "Well, it sounds like fun. I haven't been out to a movie myself for quite some time," her mother said.

"Well, if you really want to, why don't you get dressed and come along with Baron and me?" Marie suggested.

"Oh, no, Honey. I'd feel out of place."

"You wouldn't be out of place. We're only friends."

"I wish I had a friend that sent me roses. I'd go to the moon with him, if he asked. I'm only kidding, sweetheart, but I don't feel up to a movie tonight. I'll catch it some day at an early matinee. You two go and enjoy yourselves."

Baron arrived at seven thirty sharp, and Marie was dressed and ready to go. On the way to the movie, Marie asked, "If I had decided not to go with you, what would you have done?"

"I would have spent a lovely evening with you and your mother at your house," Baron said.

"Well, what if I didn't want you to?"

"Then I would have gone home and spent the rest of the night talking to you on the telephone. Before your curiosity gets the best of you, I didn't mean to make you feel that I was taking you for granted. I figured that if you didn't want to go to the movie you would have returned my call, and then I would have had a chance to ask you if I could come over and visit you for a while. So you see, the movie was just an avenue to get to see you." Marie smiled and moved close to Baron and placed her hand on his leg.

The movie was over at ten o'clock, and Baron drove Marie home. He walked Marie to her door and said; "I know it's getting late, so I won't keep you out long. Before I let you go, may I kiss you goodnight?"

When Marie looked into his eyes, she saw that he was serious, so she gave him a kiss on the cheek. Baron looked into Marie's eyes and said, "You kissed me, now let me kiss you."

He gently pulled her close to him, put his arms around her, and kissed her lips. He pulled away, and Marie's lips chased his. He kissed her lips, and she sucked his tongue. After minutes of kissing and caressing, Baron said, "I'm going to let you go now because I'm tempted to go further, and I don't want these moments to end in a rush. I'll hold the memory of tonight until a more convenient time."

Baron blew a kiss at her as he drove away. Marie went inside still tasting his delicious kisses.

The thought of him lingered on her mind as she prepared herself for bed. As she got under the covers, she was reminded of what she had been missing. She placed her hand between her legs, and the more she thought about Baron pushing his body against hers, the hotter she became. She rolled over on her back and pulled down her panties. She closed her eyes and imagined that she was in bed with Baron and that he was on top of her, moving his body over hers. She placed her middle finger between her legs and began to gently rub her vagina. The more she rubbed, the better she felt. Marie became wet, and she whispered Baron's name. Finally, she lay breathless and thought; *I can't go on like this. I don't know how long I'm going to be able to hold out. I need the real thing, and I want Baron to give it to me.*

Chapter 13

Marie woke up the next morning feeling unsatisfied. She longed for the intimate love that Baron could give her. She was frustrated and grumpy. When lunchtime came, she didn't want to go to the cafeteria, but she knew if she didn't go, Ann and Jean would think there was something wrong, and they would come looking for her. Marie tried very hard to get in the mood and pretend to be happy. She said to herself, *I vowed not to let a man get this close to me again. I've got to snap out of this.*

Marie got up and reluctantly went to the cafeteria. She sat at the table with a smile and pretended to enjoy her meal. After lunch she went back to her office. Thoughts of Baron raced around in her head, and she couldn't concentrate on her work. By the end of the day, she was drained. She went straight to her room and lay across the bed.

Marie's mother came into her bedroom and asked, "Is there anything wrong, dear?"

Marie put her arms around her mother's neck and said, "Oh Mom, I don't know. I just don't know."

Mrs. Mason stroked Marie's hair and said, "Let's talk about it. Did something happen today?"

"No, it's not that. I vowed that I'd never again let a man get as close to me as I let Robert get. Now I find myself feeling those same feelings for Baron when I was in love with Robert."

Her mother asked, "These feelings, do they make you feel good or bad?" "Well, good in the way that I feel when I'm with Baron and bad when I think of the way I'm going to feel if I'm in love with him and he leaves me."

"Don't worry, sweetheart. Right now, you're confused, and I guess you should be after all you've been through. But take your mother's advice and hold out for as long as you can. Then just follow your heart and let God be your guide. Stop dwelling so much in the past; try to keep some of the good memories instead of feeling hurt thinking about the bad ones. Things have changed. We've all changed in some way or another. You should stop basing things on your bad experiences and try to open your heart to something new."

"You're right. I guess I'm just letting my thoughts get out of control." Marie hugged her Mom and said, "Thanks for helping me get my mind together."

Her mother smiled and said, "You just remember, no matter what happens I'll always be here for you." She held Marie's shoulders and said, "Don't worry. Everything is going to be all right. Just you wait and see."

Marie had no problem getting her divorce. It was almost automatic because no one knew where Robert was. Marie's attorney placed the request for divorce in the newspaper for a long time, and since no one contested the divorce, Marie was granted one. Marie had no intentions of ever marrying again. As for falling in love, well, she would wait and see what happened.

Baron and Marie began to see each other frequently. Each time they went on a date, Baron would stop by Marie's house to pick her up. Sometimes they would have dinner at Marie's house with her mother. He was always on time, and he was always a gentleman. After about three months of dating, when Baron picked up Marie for dinner, she asked, "Where are we going tonight?"

"You'll see," said Baron. "It's a surprise."

Baron drove to a quiet neighborhood where the houses were beautiful. He stopped at a little, light blue house that had a white picket fence around it. "Is this where we're having dinner? Is this your house?" Marie asked.

"Yes," said Baron, "and I'm doing the cooking." He walked around the car to open the door for Marie.

They walked to the front door of the house. Baron opened the door and said, "Welcome to my home."

As Marie walked inside, she looked around and saw how beautiful the house was. She smiled and said, "I didn't expect to have to cook tonight, but if I do, I don't mind."

"No, you don't have to cook tonight. Dinner is almost ready. All that's left for me to do is warm it up and serve it."

Baron escorted Marie to the couch, and as Marie sat down, he asked if he could get her something to drink. "Yes, that would be nice," she said, so Baron brought her a glass of wine. Then he went into the kitchen to prepare dinner. When the food was hot, he set the table in the dining room with two candles, a dish of rib eye steaks, green beans, salad, and strawberry shortcake for dessert—all of which had been catered.

He went into the living room, held out his hand to Marie, and said, "Dinner is served." Marie took Baron's hand and they went into the dining room.

When Marie saw the way Baron had set the table, she said, "Oh, this is so nice." Baron pulled a chair out for Marie. He went to the refrigerator and got two glasses and a bottle of wine. He filled the glasses before setting them on the table and sat in a chair across from Marie. Soft music played in the living room. When they finished, Marie told Baron how delicious the dinner was.

"I'm glad you enjoyed it," Baron said, smiling.

When he got up to gather the dishes, Marie said, "Oh, no you don't." She grabbed the dishes from his hand and said, "Don't even try it." She placed the dishes back on the table and led him into the living room.

"Sit here on the couch; it's your turn to relax," she said. "You watch TV while I do the dishes." She placed the remote in his hand.

"Well, if you say so," Baron said, as he leaned back on the couch. Marie went into the kitchen and began to do the dishes. When she was finished, she went into the living room and sat

beside Baron. They held each other's hand as they watched TV. During love scenes in the movie, they squeezed each other's hand and before the movie ended they kissed. The couch seemed too small so they rolled onto the carpet in front of the fireplace. They kissed and caressed, becoming more passionate. Marie had been waiting for six months, and she refused to wait any longer. She pulled down her panties and placed Baron's hand between her legs. Baron began to rub her vagina gently and felt a wetness flowing from Marie's body.

His finger slipped inside her. Marie moaned as she placed her hand on Baron's zipper. He assisted Marie in unzipping his pants. Marie couldn't wait for Baron to unbuckle his belt so she pulled his pants down; she reached inside, and grabbed Baron with her hand. She squeezed and rubbed it, and then she pulled his body close to her and said, "Put it in! Oh, please, put it in." Baron reached down with his hand and led himself into her. He began to stroke in and out of her. "Give it to me! Oh, give it to me! It feels so good," Marie said, tears rolling down her face. "It's just like I thought it would be. Oh, Baron, I love you so much."

"I love you, too," Baron said hoarsely.

They both cried out with pleasure when they reached climax. They lay exhausted and satisfied in front of the fireplace. With Marie's legs open and Baron lying between them, they fell asleep.

When Marie woke up, she looked at the clock and saw that it was 2 A.M. "Baron," she said, shaking him. "Wake up. I have to go now. Mom will be worried. I didn't tell her I was going to stay out all night."

Baron got up and went into the bathroom to get himself together. When he returned, he asked, "Would you like to use the phone to call your mother and let her know you're okay?"

"If she's asleep, then the call would wake her up. I'll just go into the house quietly."

After Marie and Baron got dressed, Baron drove her home. When they arrived, Baron got out and walked Marie to her door. He kissed her and said goodnight. "I'll call you tomorrow," he said. He walked back to his car, waited until Marie was inside, and then he drove away.

Baron and Marie dated for a year, and they fell deeper and deeper in love. Marie spent all her weekends with Baron at his home. When Friday came and Marie finished work, she would go home and pack enough clothes to last the weekend. She would kiss her mom and tell her that she was going to be at Baron's house.

Baron played the lottery every Friday when he got his paycheck. The lottery numbers were shown on television on Saturday. Baron had been so busy with Marie that one weekend he forgot to check his numbers and left the lottery tickets in his shirt pocket. Before leaving for work on Monday, Baron gathered his clothes to take them to the laundry after work. He shook his shirt, and his lottery tickets fell out. Baron picked them up and placed them on a shelf in the laundry room and continued to gather up his dirty laundry. Some nights later, after Baron and Marie made love, he told Marie that he loved her and wanted to spend the rest of his life with her. "I want to marry you," Baron said seriously.

Marie told him that she didn't think she was ready for marriage. She said she wouldn't even think about marriage until she had saved enough money to take care of them in case something happened, or if they decided to have a child after they were married. "I know you love me, and I

love you just as much," she said, "but I'm afraid if we got married, things would change between us, and to lose you would mean going through hell all over again."

"Okay, I won't rush you," Baron said.

Three more months passed. On a Thursday, when Baron came home from work, he thought about what he and Marie could do during the weekend. He took off his work clothes to get comfortable. When he was undressed he thought, *I'll just bundle all my clothes together now instead of waiting until Monday.*

He grabbed his work clothes and went into the laundry. When he looked on the shelf, he saw some old lottery tickets. He picked them up and looked at the date and saw that they were three months old. Baron took them out of the laundry room and placed them on the table near the telephone. Then changed into more comfortable clothes and went into the kitchen for a beer.

When he returned to the living room, he decided to call the lottery office and check the tickets before he forgot about them again. Baron called the lottery office and got the winning numbers for the date that the tickets were purchased. He listened to the numbers and examined his tickets. After he hung up the phone, Baron stared at the ticket and then yelled, "Oh, Lord Jesus, I'm rich!"

Chapter 14

The lottery was worth $5,000,000. Baron paced the floor until he was able to think what to do next. He called the lottery office again to be sure of the numbers. The winner's instructions were on the back of the lottery tickets. Baron read every word to make sure he did everything correctly. He was so excited that he got dressed and went downtown and rented a room in a hotel that was on the same street as the lottery office to be sure that he would be there when the office opened the next morning. Baron lay in the hotel room, fantasizing about what he was going to do when they gave him the lottery money.

Baron woke up the next morning at ten. He rushed to the bathroom and washed his face. Quickly he went to his car and drove to the lottery office. He could hardly believe what he was doing. When he walked into the building, the receptionist directed him to the fifth floor. Once there, he presented the ticket with his name on it to the receptionist. She smiled and asked Baron to have a seat and told him someone would be with him in a few minutes. Baron tried to sit patiently, but he was nearly bursting with excitement.

A man dressed in a dark suit came to greet him. The man asked Baron if he had a driver's license and a credit card for identification, plus the winning ticket. Baron reached into his pocket and pulled out the necessary items.

"Follow me," the man said.

He led Baron to a conference room where arrangements for paying fees were discussed. Baron was given copies of all the papers that he signed, in case he wanted to consult an attorney as to their authenticity. When Baron left the room, he had in his hands a cashier's check for the sum of a million dollars and agreement papers for the rest of the money to be paid in installments.

"Mr. Shoulders," the receptionist said, "we have a car waiting for you outside to take you home, or to the bank, if you like."

"I have my car outside," Baron said, confused.

"We recommend that you leave your car parked and come back later to get it since you're carrying so much money on you. It's for security protection."

"Oh, thank you very much," Baron said. He walked out of the office and thought. *This is going to take some getting used to.*

"Where do you wish to go first?" asked the driver.

Baron remained silent. The driver said, "Home or the bank, Mr. Shoulders?" Baron snapped out of it and said, "The bank, please." He told the driver the name of his bank.

When they arrived at the bank, Baron got out of the car and went inside. When he came out, he had twenty thousand dollars in cash, a credit card with a five hundred thousand dollar limit, and a checkbook for an account containing the remainder of the million.

With a smile on his face, he said, "Take me home now, driver." He gave the driver directions for getting to his house. When they arrived, Baron thanked the driver and then gave him a hundred dollar bill.

"Thank you, Mr. Shoulders," said the driver, and he drove away. Baron walked to his front door, opened it, and went inside. He flopped down on the couch and began to think about what he wanted to do first. *Now,* he thought, *all those places I've ever dreamed of going to, I can, and all those things I've ever dreamed of doing, I can do. I'm going to marry Marie, regardless of how she feels.*

He called a cab and asked the driver to take him to the lottery office to pick up his car. When Baron got into his car, he headed for a jewelry store to find an engagement ring for Marie. In the store he looked into the glass case, saw what he thought was the perfect set of wedding rings, and asked the store salesman to take them out of the case so he could see them better.

Baron was wearing an old, wrinkled T-shirt, a pair of slacks that looked like they had been slept in for days, and sneakers that looked like they used to be white. He thought if he dressed like this no one would think that he was carrying so much money. The salesman looked at Baron and said, "Are you sure I can't show you another set that's a little less expensive?"

"I want to see those," Baron said boldly.

"Yes, sir," the salesman said. He removed the set from the glass case and presented them to Baron. "They're authentic, with fine diamonds. A beautiful piece of work, I must say."

"And the price?" Baron asked.

"Well, for you, sir, I couldn't sell them for less than fifteen thousand dollars." "I'll give you twelve thousand and not a penny more." Baron said.

The salesman told Baron to wait for a moment while he consulted with his manager and went to the back of the store. The store manager came out and said, "I understand that you want to purchase this set of wedding rings?"

"Yes, I do," said Baron.

"By what means do you intend to pay for them, on a payment plan or cash?" Suspicion and arrogance dripped from his words.

"I'll buy them, but on two conditions," Baron said. "And what are the conditions?" the manager asked skeptically. "Well, the first condition is that you take twelve thousand dollars for them, and the second condition is that you give them to me now as they are."

"Excuse me, but how did you say that you were going to pay for these rings?" "By credit card," said Baron, as he passed the card to the manager. The manager slowly reached out for the credit card and gave it to the clerk to process. When the amount cleared the bank, he rushed back to Baron and shook his hand. Now that the sale was made, his entire demeanor was transformed. "Yes, Mr. Baron, this is very nice. I'm so glad to be doing business with you. Here are your rings," and he passed over two black boxes. "If there is anything more we can do for you, please, please, let us know."

Baron walked out of the store and headed for his house. Along the way, he stopped at a flower shop and ordered twenty dozen roses to be sent to Marie's office before she left work, with a card that read, *I'm going to marry you, no matter what. Love always, Baron.*

When Baron got home, he called a limousine service and ordered a limo to pick Marie up from work and bring her to his house. Three florists brought the roses into the building where Marie worked. They asked the receptionist where Mrs. Maxwell's office was, and the receptionist gave them directions. When they got to Marie's office, they knocked on the door.

"It's open," Marie said.

One of the florists said, "I have a delivery for Mrs. Maxwell." "I'm Miss Maxwell."

The florist set the vase with a dozen roses in it on Marie's desk. Marie looked down to sign the receipt. "I have more for you, ma'am," the florist said. She looked up and saw the other florists pushing carts containing the other nineteen vases.

"Oh, my God. What is this? Are you sure you have the right place?" The last florist said, "You are Mrs. Maxwell, aren't you?" "Yes," Marie said slowly.

"Then these are yours. Where would you like them?" Vases were placed on tables, counters, and across her desk. The office was bathed in the fragrance of roses. When they were all placed, the florist picked up the receipt Marie had signed and said, "Good day, Mrs. Maxwell. Enjoy your roses."

***I'm going to have to rent a small U-haul van to carry the roses to my house,* Marie thought. She looked at the card and saw that the flowers were from Baron. *Has he lost his mind? If he wants to marry me that badly, I better let him before he goes broke trying to win me! We could have used some of that money to go on a honeymoon or something!* She paused. *Honeymoon!* She shook her head. *What am I thinking?* Even though Marie thought that she wasn't ready for marriage yet, Baron's actions were quickly changing her mind.**

Before she left the building, the receptionist stopped her and told her that a limousine parked outside was for her.

"What?" Marie exclaimed. "Can you tell me what this is all about?" "I don't know. The

driver said to let you know he would be waiting for you when you got off work."

"Well, I'm going to get to the bottom of this. This is really too much." Marie went outside and asked the driver who sent the limousine.

The driver replied, "Mr. Shoulders sent it." He opened the door for her and said, "Shall we go?"

Marie looked at the driver and asked, "Where are we going?" "To Mr. Shoulders' house."

He closed the door behind Marie and walked around to the other side of the limousine. As the driver pulled away, Marie thought, *there must be something wrong with Baron.*

The driver drove straight to Baron's house. The driver got out and opened the door for Marie. Marie rushed up the walkway to Baron's front door and rang the doorbell. When Baron opened the door, he opened it just enough to get his hand and arm out.

He handed the little black box to Marie and spoke through the crack in the door. "You can't come in unless you say yes."

Marie took the box and looked into it. "Look at the diamonds on this ring!" "It's yours if you say yes," Baron said, teasingly.

"I'm not going to say anything until you open this door, Baron Shoulders." Baron opened the door and put his arms around Marie. He escorted her inside and Said, "I was only kidding. I was going to let you in, but first I wanted to see how you'd react to the ring." They walked over to the couch and sat down.

Baron got down on his knees and said, "Marie, I want to marry you. I love you so much, and I want to share the rest of my days with you. Please marry me." He took Marie's ring finger and gently placed the engagement ring on it.

Marie was in a daze. She looked at the diamonds glittering brightly. "This is too much. What's on your mind? First of all, you don't call me last night, then you send twenty dozen roses to my office, a limousine to pick me up, and now you give me an engagement ring that only the governor could afford? Then, to top it all off, you ask me to marry you. Is this a joke or something? Because if it is, I can't handle it," Marie said, her voice quivering.

"No, it's not a joke," Baron said. "I sent you the roses because that's how much I love you, and I wanted to apologize for not calling you last night. I sent the limousine because we have a lot to do to prepare for our wedding, and if we don't have to drive, we can concentrate on other things. After all, it's not every day that you get married."

"Okay, this whole thing still sounds crazy to me. And I'm crazy enough to say yes. I love you, and I'm going to marry you, but you must promise me that you'll stop spending money like this. Did you stop to think how much those roses cost? That was enough money for us to take a honeymoon. I'm sure you could have used that money for something else. Look how many years it's going to take you to pay for this wedding ring. If we get into too much debt now, we can't do anything or borrow anything once we're married."

Baron said, "Okay, Marie, can you stop talking for a minute and listen to me?" "Yes," Marie said.

"Okay, here it is in a nutshell. I love you, and I want to marry you and take care of the both of us for the rest of our lives. I don't want you to worry about paying bills. I want you to quit your job and take care of the house and a little one, if there is a little one. I guess what I'm really trying to say is that I want you to be happy, and I want you to be happy with me and let me make some of your dreams come true."

"But Baron, if I quit my job, are you financially able to take care of us and our bills?"

"Yes. Just trust me, and you'll never regret it. Now come on, let's not discuss this any longer. Let's just go and tell your mother about our decision to get married." Baron grabbed Marie's hand and walked her to the front door.

"What are we going to do about the flowers in my office and the limousine?" Marie asked.

Baron said, "Don't worry, sweetheart. I'll take care of that." Baron gave the limousine driver Marie's address and told him to go to her office and pick up the roses and take them to her house. Marie and Baron got into his car and drove to Marie's house to tell her mother the good news. When they arrived, Baron got out of the car and opened the door for Marie. They walked up to the front door with their arms around each other. Marie took out her keys and opened the door, and they both went inside.

"Have a seat," Marie said to Baron. She went into the kitchen looking for her mother, calling "Mom, I'm home."

She heard her mother say, "I'm in the den, sweetheart."

Marie went into the den and said, "Oh, Mom, look!" She held out her hand to show her mother the beautiful engagement ring.

"Oh, baby, that's beautiful" her mother said. She pulled Marie's hand closer to get a better look. "That ring must have cost a fortune. Did Baron give you that?"

"Yes. He asked me to marry him, and I said yes."

"Where is he?"

"He's in the living room," said Marie. "Well, have him come back here."

Marie kissed her mother on the cheek. Marie went into the living room and grabbed Baron's hand. "Come on." She led him into the den.

"Have a seat and make yourself at home," said Mrs. Mason. "So, when do you two plan to get married?"

"Well, we haven't set the date yet, but I hope it'll be soon," Baron said. "I'm happy for both of you. I think you're two nice people, and you deserve each other.
I wish both of you all the happiness that life together can bring."

"Thank you, Mrs. Mason," said Baron.

"You may as well start calling me Mom." "Excuse me, Mom," Baron smiled.

He turned toward Marie and asked, "Can we go do some planning for our wedding now?"

Marie knew that was her cue for a conference with Baron, so she said, "We're going to Baron's house now, Mom. I'll talk to you later."

Baron stood up and said, "Well, see you later, Mom."

They walked out of the den and headed toward the front door. Mrs. Mason yelled, "If you need me for anything, just let me know."

On the way to Baron's home, he said, "Now that you've agreed to marry me, I think I should tell you that I'm a millionaire." Marie was silent for a few minutes as she thought of all the hardships that she had experienced in life. It hadn't been easy for her. She always had to work for everything she got. She asked, "Did I hear you say that you're a millionaire?" He told her that she had heard him correctly.

"Oh, my God!" It was going to be strange not having to wake up early and go to work. It was going to be hard for her to get used to that kind of life. But she was definitely going to give it a try.

Chapter 15

After the wedding, Baron and Marie lived happily, enjoying the best that money could buy, but Marie had become bored with having everything at her fingertips and people waiting on her hand and foot. She felt depressed, and even though there were a lot of people around her, she still felt alone. Baron had invested large sums of money into different companies, so he spent a lot of time at board meetings and traveling. Marie could travel with Baron whenever she wanted to, but she still felt lonely, especially when Baron would be tied up at some meeting or another.

One night while in their hotel suite, Marie talked to Baron about her feelings. She told him that she felt bored and lonely and couldn't keep herself occupied.

"Well sweetheart, maybe you should try some kind of therapy to help relax your mind."

"You know, that's a good idea, but I think a trip to visit relatives might do me more good," Marie said, as she gave Baron a kiss. Marie had a cousin named Sara who was one of her favorite people. When Baron was getting ready for his next business trip, he asked Marie if she would like to come along.

"Not this time, honey. I want to go and spend the weekend with my cousin." "Okay, sounds great. I think you should get out more anyway. It will do you some good. At least it should keep you from being bored here at home."

"You are so understanding. I love you," Marie said, as she gave Baron a kiss. Baron left for his trip, and Marie packed a bag to visit her hometown. One of her first stops was at her cousin Sara's house.

Sara was married, but she and her husband weren't getting along well. They were constantly arguing, and Sara suspected her husband, Mac, of cheating on her. Whenever she confronted him about it, he denied it. He always said that he didn't want to argue with her and would leave the house. Mac did not have a normal past and he refuses to talk much about his past to Sara.

Mac grew up in a mansion owned by his grandmother whom at the time he was growing up she was thought by Mac to be his mother and Mac's real mother Liz was thought by him to be his sister. The reason for this was that Mac's mother was only fourteen years old when she got pregnant by a wealthy married older businessman who her mother was dating at the time. One evening when the wealthy businessman came over to visit her mother he saw Liz, her daughter and Mac's mother who was fourteen years old at the time and fell in love with her innocent natural beauty. She was five foot nine inches tall and very full figured to be only fourteen years old. But Liz was a bit slow and some might say she was somewhat retarded but there were no records to prove that fact. It was as though he had become obsessed with her. On his next visit to see Liz's mother he inquired as to how the rest of her family was doing including her fourteen-year-old daughter Liz. Then he made plans to take Liz and her mother on a picnic while keeping his eyes on Liz every chance that he got. It had gotten to a point where he didn't miss a visit without making some excuse to see or be with Liz. At that time, Liz's mother didn't suspect anything because after all he was a married man and he wasn't married to her.

Mr. Osier, the married businessman had begun thinking that he had to have Liz and he wanted her badly he didn't care who go hurt or how much money it would cost him, he had to have her. Mr. Osier knew that when he and Liz's mother went out on a date Liz would be left at home alone. So one evening when he had planned a date for him and Liz's mother, he sent a car for Liz's mother and had the car to take her thirty miles away from where she lived to a discreet fancy restaurant that had a table reserved for two in Mr. Osier's name. Liz's mother was supposed to wait there until he arrived. But what her mother didn't know was that Mr. Osier had planned the restaurant outing so he could try to go to her apartment and be with her fourteen-year-old daughter and it worked. Mr. Osier went to Liz's mother's house and rang the doorbell knowing that her mother wasn't at home. Liz was in her night cloths as she yelled, who is it? It's me Liz. Mr. Osier he said with a happy as usual voice. Liz thought it was ok to let him in because he seem like a father figure to her and after all he was always doing nice things for her and her mother.

So Liz let him in and as usual when he came over he poked fun at Liz and got her laughing. Liz thought it was funny that he never asked for her mother but she didn't say anything because everything seem so normal to her. Then he sat on the couch next to Liz and said, let play a game if you win I will give you twenty dollars but if you lose you have to do something for me. To Liz this seem like a game that she could win besides he always gave her and her mother money anyway. So Liz played the game of matching fingers, the first five times she won and each time he gave her twenty dollars. Liz had won one hundred dollars and that was more money than she had ever had in her hand at once so she was very excited then she lost a match and Mr. Osier said I want to save this win until I win twice. Ok, sounds good to me Liz said as she won another match and twenty more dollars. Mr. Osier finally won a second match then he said well since you now owe me two matches you have to let me pinch your cheeks twice and with a smile on her face Liz said ok and Mr. Osier gently pinched both of her cheeks. Soon Mr. Osier was winning lots of matches and pinching Liz gently in different places on her face and body. Mr. Osier looked at his watch. Then he said we have to keep our game a secret because if you tell your mother she won't let me give you any more money. And Liz agreed.

Ok, I'm going to go and get your mother now but remember don't tell her that I have already been here playing games with you I'll be back soon said Mr. Osier. Then he left Liz's apartment and sped away headed for the restaurant where Liz's mother was waiting. When he arrived he apologized for being late and used having a problem with his wife as an excuse. Liz's mother once worked for Mr. Osier part time so she knew that he was a cheater but she didn't care as long as he paid the bills and kept her and her daughter living nice. Several times a car was sent for Liz's mother and each time Mr. Osier would visit Liz to give her money and play games with her until one night the games got dead serious, Mr. Osier couldn't stand it any longer he wanted Liz and he had to have her. So this time when he won a game he said "Now" I'm going to give yon one hundred dollars but you have to let me kiss you on the lip. Liz had gotten use to him pinching and touching her so she said; "ok" it's a deal.

So Mr. Osier leaned over, placed his hand on Liz's thigh and kissed her on the lip. He enjoyed the kiss so much until he wanted to kiss her again then he said ok Liz that was good but I'm going to give you another hundred dollars if when I kiss you, you suck my tongue and with a smile still on her face she said ok deal. Mr. Osier gave Liz the hundred dollars and she began sucking his tongue when he kissed her. Liz began to feel funny inside; her kisses became wet and moist as she sucked on Mr. Osier's tongue. Mr. Osier kept rubbing Liz's thighs as she kissed him. Soon he had his hands between her legs and touching her muffs as she began to breath hard, he could feel that Liz was very wet and ready so he didn't hesitate to lead her down on the couch, open her legs, place himself inside her and began stroking her. Liz wasn't a virgin and because of her size she attracted boys older than she was and they had been having sex often. And her mother knew nothing about this. But to Mr. Osier it seems like it was the very first time and she was his virgin. Mr. Osier didn't know it but Liz would share all of the money that he gave her with her friends drinking beer and smoking pot most of the time. But finally he had gotten what he wanted from Liz and the games were soon over. But what Mr. Osier didn't know was that when he had sex with Liz she got pregnant. And by the time her mother found out it was too late for an abortion.

Liz's mother pleaded and begged Liz to tell her who the father was but Liz didn't really know because she had sex with lots of guys her age and older. So one night when Liz and her mother were arguing her mother asked. Who have you been fucking? And in an angry voice Liz responded without thought, Mr. Osier, I've been fucking Mr. Osier Liz said as she began to cry. For a moment her mother was speechless then she yelled, why you little bitch, don't you dare try to blame this on my man and her mother slapped her. Liz cried even louder as she said its true mom its true he game me money to do it with him. Her mother gathered her senses as she thought, that bastard, he's going to pay for this big time. And Liz's mother grabbed the telephone and called Mr. Osier on his private line. Harry, we need to talk its an emergency her mother said. Mr. Osier made arrangement to meet with Liz's mother discreetly at a hotel near by. When they were inside the hotel room Liz's mother said I knew that you were a cheater but this time you went too far. What do you mean honey asked Mr. Osier. My daughter is pregnant and she's been fucking you.

"Oh, no, it must be someone else she's been fucking not me said Mr. Osier. Do I need to have you take a blood test asked Liz's mother. Oh, no, please don't, I'll give you anything that you want. If word got out about this it would ruin my life with my family and business. Mr. Osier said sadly. Liz's mother knew then that Liz was telling the truth and Mr. Osier was the father of her soon to be grandchild. And before he could say another work Liz's mother said I want a house, a house big enough to raise my grandson in. Ok you can have one of my mansions; I'll have the deeds made over to you tomorrow and no one has to know about it he said. "We will also need furniture Liz's mother said. Ok I'll have it all ready for you when you get ready to move let me know and I will get you some furniture Mr. Osier said.

When their talk was over as Liz's mother left the room she said, I don't want you to ever have anything else to do with my daughter again. Ok I won't I promise I won't, it was a mistake in the beginning anyway. I was drunk; he said. And Liz's mother slammed the door on her way out. Liz and her mother kept quiet about her pregnancy and when the child was born Liz gave the child to her mother. And never claimed it as her son. Her mother told her sisters and everyone else in the family that Mac was her child born out of wedlock by a rich businessman. This allowed Liz to continue to grow even wilder than she already was. At the age of seventeen when Mac was only five years old she allowed him to see her do things with boys and men that he didn't understand until he was almost grown and all that time Mac thought that his mother was his sister. Mr. Osier was

allowed to see his son but only from a distance, he couldn't risk anyone finding out that Mac was his son. But he took good care of Mac, Liz, and Liz's mother. So good that Liz was spoiled to the point that money was no object with her.

She threw money around like it meant nothing to her, there were times that she would have sex with a guy right in front of Mac who was becoming a teenager and who still thought that she was his sister. Whenever Mac would catch her doing something that he thought was wrong he would tell his mother who was really his grandmother and she would always tell Mac not to worry she would get on Liz about what she was doing. Liz became an alcoholic but she was an alcoholic who had money and lots of it. Every week when she checked her mailbox there would be from one to five thousand dollars cash money for her from Mr. Osier. This is why she kept her mouth shut and kept spending the money. Sometimes that she would take Mac shopping and buy him very expensive cloths, shoes and watches. Mac would always be happy when he came home and told his mother what Liz had bought him and although she started to do so many times, Liz never told Mac that she was his real mother. Soon Mac was twenty years old and his real mother had been in and out of treatment centers for alcoholics and finally out of the blue she stopped drinking.

Mac and Liz's mother couldn't believe it but they accepted it with joy. The thing that Liz vowed to do one day was to tell her son Mac who his real mother and father is. But before she could get around to telling him. His father, Mr. Osier had past and in a secret will hidden from the rest of his family he left His Son Mac the mansion that he, Liz and Liz's mother were living in and two hundred fifty thousand dollars in care of who Mac thought was his mother and who was really Mac's grandmother. But Mac wouldn't be allegeable until he was twenty-one years old or older. Mac had gone off to college and Liz's mother had grown old and was dying with cancer. She had pleaded with Liz to tell Mac who his real parents were but Liz started back drinking and she couldn't bring herself to tell him. So in a letter to her sister Liz's mother wrote and told her about Mac and who his real mother and father is and asked her sister to explain it to Mac if she died before he got back home from college that year. Liz's mother died and it was left up to her sister to tell Mac about his life and who his real mother and father is.

Liz's mother sister never liked Liz because she drank so much and she didn't like to be around her. So after Liz's mother funeral her aunt took Mac to her house and said sit down son, I have something to tell you. And she went on to say; my sister was not your real mother. Your sister is your real mother. Mac was in shock as he said, what are you saying to me aunt Evelyn? He asked with tears running down his face. She put her arms around Mac and rocked him back and forth as she said your real father was Mr. Osier a rich businessman who had sex with your real mother at a very young age so young that it would have ruined him if anyone found out about it. So he, your mother and grandmother hid it from the public's eye and he took care of the three of you for the rest of his life. Mac was angry and bitter with everyone. He didn't want to face the fact that his sister was really his mother mainly because of some of the things that he saw her do and some things that they had done together. In his second year, Mac dropped out of college and became a city transit bus driver. Then he started spending his inheritance unwisely. His mother Liz started using drugs and somehow she was able to sell the mansion and blow the money. So when Mac's money was getting low he went back looking for his mother hoping to get her to sell the mansion and split the money between the two of them.

But when Mac arrived at the mansion's gate it was locked and there was a sign posted this is property of James A Smith please keep off of this property. After searching through the neighborhood, he didn't find his mother but he stopped at the store that he and his family used and when inquiring about his mother the store manager told him that she sold the property and probably left town. Depressed and down hearted once again Mac was in despair. A year later Mac met Sara and fell deeply in love with her. They dated he proposed to her and they were married. After Mac had been married for a while he got a phone call from a woman and Sara picked up the phone. "Hello said Sara. Then who ever was on the other end hung up. Sara didn't say anything

to Mac about the call. But she suspected that he was having an affair with another woman. So the woman made the call to Mac's house again and this time Mac answered the phone. "Hello he said. Hello Mac, I know you don't know my voice but this is Liz. When Mac heard Liz he felt sad, his attitude changed and he was very angry but he listen as Liz tried to apologize for the things that she had done. Liz didn't know it but her aunt Evelyn had already told Mac about his family and by the end of her conversation she said. Mac, I need to tell you who your real mother and father is.

And with a sad voice Mac said in anger, "No Liz you don't need to tell me anything I already know who my mother and father is and I don't want to see them ever again he shouted as he hung up the phone. Sara heard the shout and came running into the room and asked. "What's wrong Mac? Then Mac calmly answered. Nothing, there is nothing wrong. And he walked out of the room. Mac was a changed man. He could never again be the person that Sara married it was as though he didn't care about anything anymore. And after all that had happened to him, the past had left its mark on him for life. At work Mac was introduced to John Casey, who was the general manager for the Bus transit and they became good friends.

John was a heavy drinker and one day he invited Mac and his wife Sara over to his house for dinner and Mac accepted. After dinner they went into the den for drinks. Mac drank three drinks as he talked to John and was getting high. John seems to be already high. Sara and Janet sat sipping their drink and making small talk with each other. Then out of the blue John said in a slurry voice, you know what Mac? I think my wife Janet likes you. Mac didn't know how to respond to that thought. It came as a shock to him. And Janet and Sara looked at each other as if to say, he's had too much to drink. But they remained quiet as John talked. "Sara" I think you and I should go into the other room and let them have each other John said. Then Janet got up and while leading Sara to the other room she said, Oh please don't pay any attention to what John is saying. He is drunk and he thinks every man wants me. So Sara and Janet sat in the living room talking while John and Mac sat in the Den drinking. Since John and Mac had become close friends John thought it was ok to share a few things about him that no one but his family knew, so while drinking he said. Mac, I have cancer and don't know how much longer I have to live. My children are ok but I can't give my wife what she needs. She's a young beautiful woman and I can't even have sex with her John said regretfully.

You are a good man, John said and I wish you could have sex with my wife for me just once, so I could know that she is lying down with a man that I know is a good man John said slurring his words as he talked. I don't know if I could do that I'm married Mac said. Oh, I know that you are married and don't have any kids I looked at your records when we hired you remember? said John as he smiled. I don't want to break up your happy home; I just want to see my wife have something good before I leave this earth. Just as John was about to say something else, Janet and Sara walked into the room and Sara said, its time for us to be leaving, I'm getting sleepy and I have to drive Mac and I home. So John and Janet walked Mac and Sara to the door. It was a very nice dinner Thanks Sara said. Yes it was said Mac as they left the house headed for their car. Don't forget what we talked about John said as he waved at them as they drove away.

On their way home Sara said, what a strange couple and some of the things that John said was terrible. What do you mean asked Mac? He said that his wife Janet liked you said Sara. Well I don't think that he meant in the sense that she liked me as an intimate friend but as a friend, friend. Mac said. All right clean it up real good for him I know what he meant and it wasn't just a friendly statement said Sara in an angry voice. Why is it that every time we go somewhere we have to argue on the way home and by the time we get home you are accusing me of anything that comes to mind? I'm tired of that Mac said in an angry voice. Yes you are tired all right, too tired to make love to me lately? Yes I know about you being tired, so tired that you can't come home after work without stopping somewhere along the way before you get home? Yeah I know about you being tired all right. Sara shouted. "See, there you go again accusing me of being out fooling around after work when I only stop at the bar for a few drinks before coming home, and that's all.

Well I want you to know that you are not fooling me, I know that you are messing around on me with another woman and when I catch you we are through, I'm leaving you, I promise you that. Said Sara. When they arrived home they got out of the car. Mac opened the door and they both went inside. Tight lipped and speechless they began to prepare the ending of their night. Sara went into the bedroom took off her cloths and went into the bathroom to put on something more comfortable while Mac sat on the couch watching the Television. When Sara came into the living room Mac got up and said I'm going to the package good store, do you want me to bring anything special back? Sara knew that this was his way to leaving the house and she knew that he wouldn't be back until the early morning hours so she said no, I don't need anything and when you come back in the morning use the other bedroom and don't wake me up please. See, there you go again, getting ready to accuse me of something that I haven't done yet. I haven't even left the house yet and already you are telling me when I'll be coming back. Why can't you just take my word, when I tell you where I'm going and let me come back when I'm suppose too said Mac. Because you never come back like you are suppose to Sara said.

When Marie rang the doorbell at Sara's house, Sara opened the door and then shouted, "Oh my God! Marie, is that really you?"

"Yes, I suppose it is," Marie said. They hugged and laughed. "Come on in here, girl, and sit down so you can tell me about what you've been doing. I'm so happy to see you," said Sara.

"I'm happy to see you, too," Marie said with a smile on her face. "We haven't seen each other in years."

"Yes, I know. It's so good to be here," Marie said. "So tell me, what brings you back to this old town?" Sara asked. "Well, my husband, Baron, had to travel to a business meeting for a few days. I didn't want to go on this trip, so I decided to come visit some of my relatives."

"It was nice of you to think of me," Sara said, and she gave Marie another hug. "Where is your luggage?"

"I have some in my rental, and the rest is at the airport."

"Well, when you're ready, I'll help you get your luggage. I know you're going to spend at least one night with me, right?" Sara asked.

"I had planned to stay at Aunt Jean's house. She already prepared a room for me." "Oh, nonsense Marie, you're spending the night with me tonight. We have a lot of catching up to do."

"Well, if you insist. I'll call Aunt Jean and let her know where I am, and then we can go get the rest of my luggage."

"Sounds like a plan to me," Sara said.

Marie and Sara chatted for a while, and then they left to go get Marie's luggage. Sara's husband, Mac, came home from work. Normally he didn't get home until dark, but that was while he had a woman on the side. Since he and his other woman weren't making it anymore, he had come home early. *I wonder where that damn Sara is,* he thought to himself. *She fusses at me about coming home late from work, and when I do come home early she's not here.* Mac opened a can of beer

and sat on the couch to watch TV and drink his beer. Shortly afterward, he fell fast asleep.

Sara and Marie made it back with the luggage. "Wait, let me open the front door first, then I'll come back and help you get your bags out of the car," Sara said.

Sara got out of the car and walked to her front door. When she opened it, she saw Mac lying on the couch sleeping and gave him a rough shove. "Get up, Mac, we have company."

"What? What did you say?" he replied and sat up.

"We have company. It's my cousin Marie. Now come and help us get her luggage from the car. She's spending the night with us." Sara rushed back outside to the car. Mac got up, put his shoes on, and trudged outside.

"Marie, I want you to meet my husband, Mac. Mac, this is my cousin Marie." Mac was almost mesmerized by how glamorous and stylish Marie looked. He held his hand out for a handshake and said, "How do you do? Welcome to our home."

"Please to meet you," Marie said. She reached into the back seat of the car to get her luggage.

Mac rushed to the other side of the car and opened the opposite door. "Hold on. Let me get your bags for you," Mac said, and he reached in and began pulling out her luggage.

Afterward they sat and talked for a while. Mac got up, excused himself, and went into the bedroom. Marie couldn't help but notice that Mac was a handsome man, so she complimented Sara saying, "You sure know how to pick a man. He is very handsome, but not as handsome as my husband." They both laughed.

Mac called Sara to the bedroom, and when she got there, she noticed that Mac had gotten dressed. "I'm going to the package store to get some more beer. Do you want me to get something different for you and Marie?"

"No, we have some bottles behind the bar, and I think that's enough." Normally, if Mac said that he was going to the package store, Sara would have said not to wake her up when he got back because she knew that he would be gone until after midnight. But this time she didn't say that because she didn't want to start an argument with a guest in their home.

Sara went back into the living room and said, "Mac is going to the store for beer." Sara and Marie talked until they got sleepy then went to bed. They didn't hear when Mac came home, but it was three o'clock in the morning, and he slept on the couch so they wouldn't know what time he came in. At eight o'clock the next morning Marie and Sara were up and dressed. Sara helped Marie put her luggage into the car. "I'll call you before I leave town. Tell Mac I said thanks."

"Okay, see ya'," Sara said as Marie drove away. Afterward Sara went back inside. Mac was awake. "I see that you slept on the couch last night. I know that you did it because you didn't want me to know what time you came in," Sara said accusingly.

"No, that's not it. I slept on the couch because I didn't know which bed to get into. I looked into both rooms, and you and Marie had your heads covered up. I didn't want to get in bed with the wrong person, so I slept on the couch."

"Oh shut up, Mac, just shut up. You are such a liar. You think that I don't know that you have another woman on the side, but you're dead wrong. I know that she's the reason why you're late coming home from work, and I know she's the reason that you stay out late at night. I'm no fool, and I'm going to get my divorce. I want a man like Marie has, and you're nothing like him" Sara said. Sara went into the bathroom and began to cry.

Marie received a warm welcome at her elderly aunt's house. She got settled, and she and her aunt sat and talked. In the middle of the afternoon, her aunt went to her bedroom for a nap. Marie looked around the living room at some old photos and went outside in the yard where she played when she was a child. She wanted to see if there were any changes made to the town while she was away. She wrote a note to let her aunt know that she was going for a ride around town. Marie began to cruise the streets, remembering old times and looking at old buildings. She arrived at an old neighborhood near the school that she attended. For Marie, this was where life started and where she learned to smoke and drink. She saw a familiar face. It was a tired and rough face, the face of Sam the guy who taught her how to smoke dope.

She slowed the car down as she passed him. "Hey baby, hold up. Don't I know you?" he yelled as Marie cruised by.

"No, you don't," and she stepped on the gas to get out of that neighborhood. She then visited the bar where she fell in love with Robert and thought about how they met and the child that miscarried. The bar was open, so she went inside and sat at the bar. The bartender came over to take her order and said, "Hey, I know you. You're Marie, Robert's date. Am I right?"

"You're right, but you're wrong. I used to be Robert's date." The bartender smiled and said, "It's been a long time since I've seen you. Have the first drink on me."

"Oh, thank you. I should come here more often. I'll have a scotch and soda, please."

While the bartender fixed her drink, she asked, "How have you been doing?" "I've been serving customers, and business has been steady. By the way, did you hear from your friend Robert?"

"No, I didn't," said Marie.

"Well, I heard on the news last week that he got busted distributing cocaine." "Oh really," Marie answered, surprised.

"Robert usually stops by here every other day, but last week I didn't see him at all," the bartender told her and passed her the drink.

Marie sat at the bar for an hour, talking to the bartender and listening to the music. Then the door opened. She turned her head to see who was coming in—it was Robert. He was sharply dressed with diamonds on his fingers and a diamond in one of his ears. When he saw Marie, he stopped. He called out, "Oh no, it can't be. Marie. Is it really you?" They looked into each other's eyes. The spark of an old flame kindled in Marie's eyes. Marie stood up and greeted him. They latched onto each other. When Marie broke off the hug, Robert said, "Let's go somewhere more private so we can talk." And with his arms still around Marie he attempted to escort her to the door.

"Wait a minute. You can't expect me to leave with you just like that. I'm a different person now," Marie said.

"Yes, I know that you're a different person, and I know that you must be married judging by the large diamond you're wearing on your finger. That's why I want to go somewhere so we can talk privately."

Marie forgot the point that she was trying to make, and Robert made it seem as if he was looking out for her best interest, so she said, "Well, since you put it that way, okay, but only for a little while. I have to get back to my aunt's house." She grabbed her purse. Robert drove Marie to his beautiful home in the suburbs of the city. Once inside Marie said, "Wow, is this your home?"

"Yes, it's all I have, and it seems as if I'm going to have to sell it soon."

Marie was concerned, so as she sat on the couch, she asked, "Why would you have to sell your home?"

"Well, it's a long story, and I didn't bring you all the way over here to talk about my problems," Robert said as he walked behind his bar. "So tell me, how have you been doing? Can I get you a drink?"

"I've been doing fine, and yes, you can get me a scotch and soda. I had two drinks at the bar, and I'm not really sure that I need another one," Marie said jokingly, "but what the hell?"

Robert wasn't the sweet guy that she once knew. He had become cold, hard, and dangerous. And he was also good at seducing females. Robert knew that Marie had a history of alcohol and drug abuse. His aim was to get her hooked on drugs again, and then use the drugs to keep her under control. While Robert was fixing Marie's drink, he put a strong dose of Valium in it. He brought the drink to Marie and coaxed her into drinking all of it. In a little while Marie was feeling very relaxed, and Robert began kissing her on her neck and lips. He gently squeezed her breast while asking her if she remembered how they made love back in the day. Marie wasn't strong enough to resist, so he pulled out a little cocaine spoon, put some cocaine on it, and pretended to snort the powder. He offered Marie some, and when she refused, he forced it on her. After He leaned into her slowly, and began kissing her on the forehead indicating how he felt. Then he gave her the kind of kiss that told her what he wanted. After kissing her and teasing her with his tongue, he slowly, gently moved toward what he wanted and looked into her eyes for the answer. He searched her with his hands and that changed her breathing pattern. He whispered sweet adorations in her ear, as his fingers walked down the path that he knew would bring ecstasy. Touching gently at first, then more demanding, in search of what he thought should be his. Asking for more with his kisses grinding her kisses to where they made her say his name, she called his name and screamed. Robert, baby, right there, yes, you know exactly what I want. Oh, yes she screamed as Robert pumped his way into a climax.

so long without drugs, the cocaine hit her fast and hard. She lost control of herself. Robert, baby, right there, yes, you know exactly what I want. Oh, yes she screamed as Robert pumped his way into a climax. They started making love on the couch and ended upstairs in the bedroom. Marie forgot about being a woman of substance and values. One snort of coke, and she was headed back to a place she had left so long ago.

Chapter 16

The next morning when Marie woke up, she was in Robert's bed with a tie-off rubber band

around her arm. Robert wasn't in bed with her. She knew what she had done, and she wanted more. Robert came back into the room and held up a small bag of heroin. "Is this what you want, baby," he crooned.

Marie reached out for the bag. "Oops, not yet," Robert said. "Not until you show me how bad you want it."

"I'll do anything you want," Marie said. Her words were slurred but eager. "Will you stay with me for a few days?"

"Yes, yes I'll stay with you. Baby, give it to me, please," she begged. Robert picked up a spoon and poured the powdered drug into it. He picked up a syringe with a needle attached to it, drew up some water, squirted some into the spoon to liquefy the powdered drug, and held the spoon over a lit candle. In a few seconds the drug was ready in liquid form. He gently grabbed Marie's arm, tightened the rubber band up around it, and injected her with the drug. Marie sighed with pleasure as he took the rubber band from around her arm. "How do you feel now, baby?" he asked.

"I feel wonderful, just wonderful," she said. He watched her for a moment while the drug worked through her system. Then he began stroking her thighs. Marie lay back on the bed to let Robert have sex with her for as many times and as long as he wanted.

For three days Marie stayed at Robert's house in and out of bed. When she wouldn't eat, he would hold the little bag that contained the drug up to her face and say,

"If you eat, you could have some." And Marie would eat even though she didn't want to. He would do the same thing when he wanted her to take a shower. On the third day he went into Marie's purse, took her plane ticket, and saw the date on it. He said, "I'm sorry, Marie baby, but it is time for you to leave. I've put a few bags, my cell phone number, and a syringe into your purse. And I don't want you to use them until you get where you're going."

"Okay, Robert," Marie said softly, as she got dressed.

When she was ready, Robert escorted her to his car, and he drove her back to the bar where her car was still parked. He kissed Marie and said, "It's time for you to go home now, baby." And as she was getting out of his car he said, "Remember, if you need me, call."

Marie got out of Robert's car and into her car. She sat and watched Robert as he drove away. She wondered what day it was and drove out of the parking lot. She pulled into a gas station for gas and went into the office to pay. While inside she looked at the cover of a newspaper and saw what day it was. Marie kept her composure until she got to her car then she shouted, "Damn, damn, damn! What am I doing?" She realized that she had been away from home for four days, and she had not called her husband or her Aunt Jean.

She didn't know what to do next, but she remembered that Robert had left drugs in her purse for her. She grabbed her purse and rushed into the ladies' room. She thought to herself, *I only need a little to help me think my way out of this situation, and then I'm not going to do this anymore.*

When she was finished, she left the ladies' room and calmly got back into her car. She began to think of what she was going to do and what excuses she was going to use. Marie grabbed her cell phone and dialed Baron's cell phone. When he answered, she said, "Hello honey, I'm so glad that I could get in touch with you this time." Before Baron could say anything she said, "I've been trying

to call you for the past four days, and no one answered your cell phone. I've been so worried."

"Calm down, honey, don't get upset, you know how these cell phones are. Sometimes they just don't work and knowing you, you probably got upset and dialed the wrong number," Baron said.

"Well, maybe so. You are so understanding honey. I love you so much, and I miss you, too. I'm not staying here any longer. I'm coming home today," Marie said in her most pitiful voice.

"Okay honey, but be careful. My flight won't get in from D.C. until ten o'clock tonight, so I should be home before you get there, and then you can tell me all about your little trip," Baron said. "Honey, in a few minutes I'm going to be driving through a tunnel, and we might get shut off. If we do, don't worry. We'll talk when you get home."

Marie called her Aunt Jean next. When her aunt picked up the phone and heard her voice, she said, "Child, where have you been? I've been so worried about you. I called Sara's house, and she told me that she hadn't seen you since you left her house. If you had waited one more day before calling me, I was going to turn you in to the police as missing."

Marie laughed and said, "I'm sorry, Aunt Jean. I didn't mean to worry you. You know how it is when you run into old friends and get to talking and drinking; you lose track of time. And it seems that they all want you to spend the night with them."

"Well, I figured that you were somewhere around here with your friends, but still, you should have called me."

"Yes, I know Aunt Jean, and I'm sorry. I'll be at your house before tomorrow for sure," said Marie.

"You haven't changed clothes. Your clothes are still here at my house." "Don't worry, I bought more clothes."

"Child, I don't know about you. Well, you be careful. That's all I can say." "Okay, Aunt Jean. I'll talk to you later."

Marie felt happy that she was back on course. All she had to do now was to get her plane ticket and her baggage and get on a plane home. She left the gas station and stopped at a nearby mall to buy the new clothes she told her aunt about. She put the old clothes in the shopping bag and wore the new clothes out of the store. Then she thought, *I should at least stop at Sara's house and let her know that I'm getting ready to go back home.* By now the effects of the drugs were wearing off. Marie was getting so sleepy that she could barely hold her eyes open. Instead of going directly to Sara's house she decided to go by her aunt's house to get her luggage.

Her aunt opened the door for her. She calmly greeted her aunt and gave her a hug. She told her aunt, "I can't stay, Aunt Jean. I just talked to Baron on my cell phone, and he wants me to leave for home today. I have just enough time to put my luggage in the car and get to the airport." Marie headed to the bedroom to get her belongings.

"Well, okay dear. It was nice of you to come see me. Next time, don't stay away so long."

"Okay, Auntie, I won't." Marie finished putting her luggage into the car. Her aunt stood in

the doorway and waved as Marie drove away. Her tiredness was really coming on strong. She struggled to keep her eyes open on the way, but she made it to the airport. When she got ready to check her baggage, she looked for her plane ticket, but she couldn't find it. *I know I put that ticket in my purse,* she thought, as she searched through her purse for it. Marie became aggravated and said, "The hell with that ticket. I'll just buy another one." She went and stood in line to buy another ticket. By the time she got to the ticket salesperson, she heard the last call to board her plane.

"I've lost my ticket. Can you please help me get another one so I can catch this flight home?"

"I'm sorry miss, but it's too late to catch that flight. They're taxing out to the runway now," the agent said.

"Damn," Marie said quietly. "Okay, what time is the next flight leaving?" The woman checked her computer and said, "The next flight going your way is at Ten A.M. tomorrow."

Now Marie was really upset. "Are you sure?" she asked.

"I'm sure. If you give me your name, I'll see if we can get you another ticket." Marie stood in line nervously while the ticket agent prepared her ticket. She got her ticket and went to the baggage area to check in all of her luggage. Then she thought, *Looks like I'll get to say goodbye to Sara after all.* She called a hotel near the airport so she wouldn't miss her flight the next morning. She checked into the hotel with no luggage and said, "Damn, now I have to buy more clothes and toiletries." Marie was tired and beginning to feel sick. She had a taste for more drugs, but she didn't have anything to fix it in. She called room service, and ordered a sandwich and coffee. She tipped the waiter who brought her food, closed the door, and grabbed the spoon that came with the coffee. She could finally get her fix. This time she injected a little more than she did the last time. She sat on the bed and thought, *now I have time to go say goodbye to Sara.*

Marie left the hotel and headed to Sara's house. She was weaving on the road. More than once, she barely missed cars that were on the other side of the road. She felt that she couldn't drive any further, so when she got to the bar where everything started, she pulled into the parking lot to take a break from driving. Marie had been sitting there ten minutes before she saw a car drive up. The man that got out of the car was Mac. He was on his way inside the bar to get a drink when Marie held her head out of her car window and yelled, "Hi, Mac."

Mac heard his name and walked over to her car. He saw that it was Marie. "Hello, Marie." She looked tired, so he asked, "Are you all right?"

"Yes, I'm okay. I just had a rough day hauling my luggage to the airport. I'm getting ready to leave, and I wanted to say goodbye to you and Sara before I left. Is she at home?"

"No, she went shopping with my mother, but they shouldn't be gone too long. If you like, you can follow me back home. I could let you in, and you can wait there for her."

"That's okay, Mac, thanks anyway."

"No, it's no problem. Besides we're only down the road. I can let you in and be right back here at the bar in no time at all."

Marie followed Mac and went inside the house. "Well, you already know where everything is so just help yourself."

"Thank you," Marie said. She flopped down on the couch, and Mac went into the other room.

She passed out on the couch in moments. When she sat down on the couch, her mini skirt had slipped up so her panties showed. Mac went into the living room to ask Marie if she wanted something to drink. When he saw the state she was in, Mac cleared his throat to make some noise, thinking that Marie would hear that he was in the room and close her legs, but she didn't move a muscle. For a few moments Mac stood in the living room admiring how fine Marie was and fantasizing how good it would feel if he could have sex with her.

Mac walked over to the bar. He poured an eight-ounce glass half full of brandy and drank all of it. He went closer to Marie and called her. "Marie, Marie," and still she didn't respond. Mac focused his eyes between her legs; he could see pubic hairs sticking out from the sides of her panties. He went over and sat on the couch beside her and called her name again. Mac knew that she wouldn't be on his couch with her legs opened like that if she could help it, but he couldn't ignore the fact that Marie was a fine woman with extremely smooth skin. He put his arm around her as in an attempt to lay her down on the couch, but he didn't try not to touch her breasts or put his hand between her inner thighs closer to her private area than he needed to. He was so involved feeling up Marie that he didn't hear Sara's car pull into the driveway.

Sara saw Mac's car and Marie's car parked in front of the house, so she figured that she didn't need her key to get inside. She walked up and opened her front door. She was stunned by what she saw. Mac was sitting on the arm of the couch with his arm around Marie's neck and his hand between her legs. Her skirt was up and her panties were showing. When Mac turned his head toward the door he had a surprised look on his face. His hand was still between Marie's legs. For a few moments Sara was speechless; it was as if what she saw couldn't reach her brain So many thoughts were running through her mind. She didn't know which thought to think first. As a result the first words that came out of her mouth were, "Oh no," and she placed her hand over her mouth and rushed into the bedroom.

"Sara, wait," yelled Mac. He went into the bedroom and came up behind Sara. She was facing the wall, holding her hand over her mouth. He walked up to her to explain what she saw. Mac didn't see her clench her fist. Sara turned and punched him in the nose. Mac staggered to the other side of the room. Sara was angry as she rushed out of the bedroom and headed into the living room to confront Marie. When she reached Marie, she finally realized that Marie was unconscious. She turned around and headed back into the bedroom to finish what she had started with Mac. He had gone into the bathroom to clean the blood from his nose when Sara pushed the door open and shouted, "What's wrong with my cousin? What did you do to her?"

Mac was angry, too. "I didn't do a damn thing to her. She passed out on the couch, and I was trying to straighten her on the couch so she wouldn't fall on the floor."

When Sara heard, this she began to calm down a little. "In the first place, what was she doing here with you?"

Mac explained that Marie was parked in the parking lot at the club when he pulled up to go in and get a drink. "She called me over to ask if you were home. She said she wanted to say goodbye to you and she was planning to fly out in the morning. I told her that you were at the mall shopping. She looked tired, so I told her that I would let her in the house where she could rest and wait for you, and she followed me home."

"What were you doing at the bar anyway? You told me that you couldn't go shopping with me because your uncle was stranded on the freeway with a flat tire, and you had to go help him."

Sara walked out of the bathroom and into the living room. She wondered what had happened to Marie. She looked to be breathing regularly and seem to be asleep, so Sara straightened Marie's skirt and got a blanket to spread over her.

While Sara was attending to Marie, Mac left the house through the garage entrance slamming the door behind him. He got into his car and burned rubber as he left. Sara sat on the side of her bed and began to cry. "I've been miserable every day since I got married. I have to get out of this relationship. I want out," she said as she cried from the bottom of her heart. She cried until she had no more tears to shed.

Two hours later, Marie came out of her unconsciousness. She sat up on the couch and realized where she was. With her head in hand she said quietly, "Oh my God, I feel terrible." She saw the blanket over her and figured that Sara had put it there, but she didn't remember seeing her cousin.

Chapter 17

Marie got up and made her way to the bathroom. Afterward, she went to Sara's bedroom and saw that she was lying across her bed sleeping peacefully. Marie gently began to stroke Sara's hair remembering how close they were in their childhood days.

Sara woke up slowly. In a tired voice Sara said, "Girl, what happened to you?" Marie explained how she had been with Robert, her ex-husband, drinking, cuddling, and having fun. She told Sara how she couldn't find her ticket and missed her flight at the airport. "I was on my way to say goodbye to you when I ran into Mac in the parking lot at the bar. He said I could come wait for you here, and the rest is history. I was so tired I passed out on the couch," Marie explained.

Sara felt somewhat better that Marie had confirmed Mac's story. This had been the first time since Sara was married she felt sure that Mac was telling the truth about something. She felt a little guilt for punching Mac in the nose, but Sara felt that she had suffered too much misery in her marriage. She had made up her mind to divorce Mac. "Girl, you know anywhere I am, you are always welcome, and I do mean always." Sara moved over to one side of the bed and said, "Lay here and rest some more." Marie and Sara lay beside each other like two kids at a sleepover.

When Marie and Sara woke up the next morning, Marie said, "Oh my God. If I don't get to the airport before ten o'clock I'm going to miss my flight again." She got up and rushed into the bathroom.

"There's an extra toothbrush in the cabinet that you can use," Sara called to her. "Okay, thanks," Marie yelled as she fixed herself up. When she was ready to leave, Marie gave Sara a hug. Sara told her, "Don't forget to call me when you get home."

When Marie finally made it home she was so happy to be back where she belonged. Baron came to the airport to pick her up, and when she saw him, she dropped her bags and ran into his arms, hugging and kissing him.

"Oh, wow, let's finish this up at home honey. We need to get your bags before someone walks off with them."

“Okay, honey. I’m just so happy to see you” Marie said, and she began to cry. “Now, now honey. It’s going to be all right. You’re home now, and I’m here with you forever.” He rocked her from side to side as he held her in his arms.

Marie got herself together and said, “I think we better get the luggage now, but I want you to know that you mean the world to me.” She kissed him once again then went to grab her bags. Once they got her luggage together, Baron tipped one of the baggage handlers to carry the luggage to his car. As soon as Marie got inside her house, she sat down on her couch. Baron sat beside her and put his arm on the back of the couch behind her head.

“So how was your trip, sweetheart?”

“Oh honey, I have so much to tell you about my trip, but I’m so tired. Can you just hold me in your arms for a while, please,” Marie asked. She leaned into him and rested her head against his chest.

“Sure, honey,” said Baron. He put his arm around her shoulder and stroked her hair. Baron held her in his arms for almost thirty minutes after Marie had fallen asleep. He slipped his arm from around her and eased her down on the couch so she could stretch out.

Marie slept for a long time on the couch while Baron watched TV upstairs. When she finally woke up, she called Baron. He didn’t hear her at first because he was absorbed by the movie that he was watching, but when she called a second time he answered, “Yes, dear?”

“Oh, that’s okay honey. You don’t have to come down. I called you because I wondered where you went. I’ll be up in a minute,” Marie said.

Marie sat on the couch trying to think of what she was going to tell Baron about her trip. Then she said, “Oh God, my purse.” She grabbed her purse and began to ramble through it looking for those little bags of cocaine that Robert had left for her. *I can’t let Baron find those bags.* Finally she found them, got up from the couch with her purse, and went down to the basement to find a place to hide the bags. She was yearning to use it, and a thought crossed her mind to throw them away, but the desire to use the drug was stronger. She shot up in the basement, even while thinking, *I can’t keep this up. I just can’t.* Her mind floated as the drugs took affect. Marie had enough drugs to last her for about a week if she didn’t get greedy. She vowed that when they were gone she would never touch them again. She hid the drugs behind the washing machine and went upstairs to her bedroom. Baron was still in the upstairs studio watching a movie.

Marie got out of her clothes, took a shower, and slipped into some sexy lingerie. Then she went to the studio room and stood in the doorway with her legs opened. “Hey, I got plans for you in the bedroom,” Marie said. She looked at him sexily and moved from side to side.

Baron turned away from the TV screen, and when he saw Marie, his mouth flew open. “Bye, bye movie,” he said. He turned off the television and got up out of his seat. He walked to the doorway, grabbed Marie in his arms, pulled her body close to his, and kissed her on the way to the bedroom. Marie gave Baron three full hours of sex. Finally, Baron had to stop. “Oh honey, you are too much. This is the best sex that we’ve had since we’ve been together.”

“Well, you can handle it, can’t you?”

Baron took a deep breath and said, “I don’t know.”

"Okay, just call my name when you've had enough," Marie said, and she started riding him again. In a little while Baron yelled, "Marie, oh Marie, baby." She gave one final squeeze, and he came inside her.

She slept on top of Baron until noon. Baron got up energetically, but Marie didn't get up with him. Baron wasn't surprised, considering the sex he had with her last night. Marie woke up as Baron was stepping out of the shower. She told Baron that she was tired, and he thought it was from sex, but she lied. The effect of the drugs in her system was wearing off, and her body was cramping for more.

Chapter 18

Marie lay in bed trying to think of a way to sneak down to the basement. She thought about the linen on the bed and decided that she needed to change it. She put on her robe, took the linen from the bed, and headed downstairs. Baron was outside on the patio doing sit-ups. Marie went straight to the basement and began to prepare her drugs. She thought she needed a little bit more than the last time. When the drug was flowing through her bloodstream, she felt better. She left the basement and went upstairs to kid around with Baron.

"Ah, you couldn't handle me last night could you, honey?" Marie teased.

Baron stopped doing sit-ups and said, "Baby, last night you were magnificent." He stood up and put his arms around her. "But you're magnificent to me every night," and he gave her a kiss. "Hey, you never told me about your trip."

"Well, there's not much to tell. I visited my aunt and cousin and saw that they were doing well. I missed you and wanted to come home. That's about it," Marie said, as she walked toward the kitchen.

"Now that the trip is over you can start on your therapy." "I'm going to get into an aerobic class next week," Marie said. "Oh, I forgot to tell you, me and a couple of guys in the neighborhood are getting together at Gary's house to watch the game at three today. I'm going to grab a towel and jog on over to Gary's house. The game should be over in about two hours."

"Okay, honey. Say hello to everyone for me," she said. As soon as Baron was out of sight, Marie went down to the basement again for a little pick-me-up.

The weekend was coming up, and Baron would be going to one of his board meetings. Marie had already decided that she wasn't going with him. She used the excuse that she wanted to work on the flowers in the yard.

That weekend, Marie used the rest of her drugs. She had Robert's cell phone number in her purse, and she called him, but his cell phone said that the number was temporarily not in service. She called five times, and it gave her the same information. Marie could feel herself getting sicker. She stayed inside for two days and didn't eat, shower, or change clothes. Each time she tried to drink water it came back up. Her mouth and skin were dry; she had circles around her eyes, and she looked like a wild woman. She didn't even lock the door when Baron left. Baron had been trying to call her since he went to the airport, but no one answered the phone.

After two days had passed and Baron couldn't get an answer at the house, he called his neighbor, Bob, and asked him if he would go next door to see if Marie was home. Bob agreed and would give him a call back. When Bob got to Marie's front door he rang the doorbell. No one

answered, so he opened the door and stuck his head inside. "Marie? Marie, it's Bob. Are you in there?" Still there was no answer.

Bob was a friend with a security officer in the area, so Bob went home and called him. He told him that he had found his neighbor's door open and asked him if he would come and investigate. Bob didn't want to call Baron back unless there was a good reason, so he decided to wait and call him after the security officer investigated.

In fifteen minutes the officer arrived, opened Marie's door, and said, "Hello, is anyone home? This is the area security. I'm inside your house." No one answered. The security officer checked the rooms on the first floor and the basement and found no one. When he went upstairs to check the rooms, he found Marie lying on her bed barely breathing. The officer pulled out his radio and called in a code for the ambulance.

The ambulance came to take Marie to the hospital. Bob asked the security officer for information, but the officer was in a hurry to get to his patrol car to clear the way for the ambulance. Bob ran inside and placed a call to Baron's cell phone. Baron was in a meeting, so he had his phone turned off.

When they got Marie to the hospital, the doctors checked her blood and found that she had a high amount of drugs in her system. After two hours of nutritional medication given through an IV she began to respond. She was afraid because she didn't know where she was. She couldn't move her arms or legs. She looked and saw that she was in restraints. She began to act wild, showing symptoms of a drug user trying to kick the habit. The drugs that she took almost destroyed her brain, and the doctors weren't sure how long she would have to stay in the hospital.

Bob went to the hospital to check on Marie. He was questioned, and he told them that her husband was out of town on a business trip and gave them the number to contact him. The hospital got in touch with Baron and told him that his wife was in the hospital in ICU. Baron left his meeting immediately and was at the hospital in four hours. The doctors filled him in on Marie's condition and what they found in her blood. When Baron asked if she would be fine, the doctor said that her survival was in God's hands. The doctor stated that if she survived, she probably would have brain damage for life.

After medical care at the hospital Marie was transferred to a mental institution for long-term treatment. During the years Baron made several trips to the hospital to visit her, but there was no change in her condition. Suffering from the lack of love and affection Baron was able to divorce Marie He met another woman and fell in love.

As for Robert, Marie's ex-husband, his court date for the distribution of cocaine had come. He was found guilty and sentenced to fifty years to life in a federal prison. Marie didn't have brain damage, and in a period of time with the help of doctors and group therapy she recovered. She went through a time of putting her life back together again and in the process met Winston Edwards who had also had a hard life and had been through similar stormy events in his early life.

www.ingramcontent.com/pod-product-compliance
Ingram Content Group UK Ltd.
Pitfield, Milton Keynes, MK11 3LW, UK
UKHW040559210726
13854UKWH00008B/1508

9 781365 972140